The Bell Ringer
& Other Holiday Tales

Raven Oak

GREY SUN
PRESS

SEATTLE

INTRODUCTION

I've always wanted to release a collection, but I never thought about one that's holiday themed until this year (2022). For many people like me—disabled and immunocompromised—the pandemic has been a lonely time, one that has no end in sight as many carry on as if everything is *normal* again. The unfortunate truth is that the pandemic has left me and many others with permanent health complications, so I've had a lot of time in the past three years to contemplate what stories and art I wished to collect.

While disabled, I know my life is full of privilege. My partner is well-employed and working from home (to protect me), a warm kitty currently sits in my lap, and while the roof needs replacing, it is still a sturdy roof over my head. Despite these boons, my own mortality has been present in my mind. *A lot.* Probably more than is healthy. I think being neurodiverse and anxious helps it along some days and others, I'm reminded that good people are out there. Life continues.

As a child, holidays were complicated. We were poor—the kind with skipped meals, too much mac & cheese, and hand-me-down clothes that were forever the wrong size. Being a proud man, my father refused most government help (though we qualiÿed) and often relied on my grandmother for money to make any sort of holiday happen.

She didn't have the money to spare, but operating as a parking garage attendant, she made more than he did as a college student. He worked three minimum-wage jobs, including one stint at a gas station during the graveyard shift. Whenever I saw him, he was either sleeping in his room or falling asleep standing up. Between the lack of money and exhaustion, holidays were quiet and lonely. Most of the time, he slept through them. I think that's why I cling so hard to the holidays now that I'm an adult with my own family. The ability to share my home, food, and gifts with others is critical to my well-being.

COVID changed that in numerous ways, beginning with the inability to see my friends—my chosen family. It's made for some lonely times. Yes, my partner and my kitties are here with me, and yes, I see my friends online and via video calls, but it's not the same. I love entertaining, be it with weekly game nights or Thanksgiving dinner. All of this has stopped for me, along with the ability to attend conventions/conferences, writing retreats, and even the grocery store. My career has slowed without in-person events and my health issues from long-COVID have made my work days very different. All of this weighs heavy on me, which you'll see in some of the stories and art included in this collection.

My writing already tends to hover in the darker areas of the soul as I question the rules as we know them. I'm forever asking *why* and *how*, so it makes sense that these stories should be collected here as we approach the holidays. While I try to give my characters a *happily-ever-after*, there's always a cost to such a thing, as there is in the real world. I don't want to depress you for the holidays, but I do want to make you think. What's really important in your life? What can you do to help others? What can you do to help the pandemic go away? What legacy do you wish to leave behind?

Some of the art throughout this collection can best be described as nightmarish, but I enjoyed every digital stroke in painting them. Painting is one way a story's words are translated between the creases of my brain and the page. The movements involved in art frees my mind from stress and allows me to be in a place where words spill out like water. I had no choice but to include these paintings alongside their stories, as I feel the stories wouldn't be the same without them.

While *The Ringers* and *Ol' St. Nick* may be familiar to you from their own previous releases, "The Bell Ringer" is a new tale that fell into my brain as I watched the beginnings of the pandemic unravel. For a time, people stayed home. They masked. They worried. They did what they could to protect those of us more vulnerable. Can we get it back? That empathy and desire to shelter others from harm?

"The Curse" came to me in a dream and told a story I've always wished to tell. Something about the idea of Santa Claus has always creeped me out in many ways, and this story was a way to explore one of those reasons.

While some may ÿnd my stories a bit dark, I hope the glimmer of hope in them helps you discover your own altruistic spirit these holidays. Goodness knows we need it.

Raven Oak
March 2023

PART I

THE BELL RINGER

"The World Tree" by Raven Oak

"The Drug Store" by Raven Oak

CHAPTER ONE

John trudged through the snow toward the pharmacy when laughter reached him. Most streetlights had given up the ghost last week, the city unwilling or unable to spare anyone to replace bulbs during a pandemic, but up ahead, national guardsmen huddled together, silhouetted in vehicle headlights. One coughed—the sound of a creature tearing its way through phlegm and tissue to escape, and John stumbled backwards.

Last year, the streets had bustled with holiday shoppers, but now, abandoned cars and trash were the guardsmen's only companions. John veered away from them.

"You there! What's your business?" a second man shouted at John.

Without stopping, John gestured toward the street's end and pulled his red scarf closer against the three face masks he wore.

Not that it mattered. None of the guards were masked. He was only protected if others masked too.

The drug store's lone light shone like a beacon for those recovered, those not yet sick, or those with nowhere else to go. John believed himself in the middle group, though his wife...

A dozen feet from Gerold's Drugs, a bell near the doorway pealed, and he flinched. Who would be ringing a bell during a pandemic?

Three feet from the door, a cane rose up to stop his forward progress. Attached to it was a vagrant Santa who reeked of sour mold.

Probably three sheets to the wind by this hour. John frowned.

Santa's dingy gray suit hung loosely across his frame as he hunched over a red kettle. "Help the needy, sir?"

The same old reply tore from John's mouth. "Get a job, you drunk."

As he stepped into the drug store, perfume mixed with bleach assaulted his nose. Most aisles lay barren as he walked, though a single bag of cough drops and a bottled 12-pack lay discarded in a corner. He grabbed both before approaching the pharmacy counter.

A sleepy woman nodded to him from behind a plastic barrier. "Home test?"

When he nodded, she fetched a small box from beneath the counter, scanned it, and waited.

He followed her on autopilot, scanning the other two items and then his phone for contactless payment.

Her face twitched as she smiled. "Thank you."

Ah! She belonged to the first group--those recovered. Or mostly. The virus left quite a laundry list of neurological boogeymen behind, from spasms to hallucinations. If all that remained was the twitch...no wonder she worked.

John fetched the test from the drawer slid his way and shoved it along with the cough drops into his pocket. "Do you have a bag?" he asked, pointing to the sports drinks.

"Been out for ages now. Sorry."

For lack of a better solution, he shoved them beneath his coat as best he could. At least his walk wasn't far.

The bell ringer was gone as the snow doubled time outside, and John picked up his pace. He needed to get back to work, assuming the snow hadn't killed the Internet. Again.

Last year, getting sick had been laughable--the virus nothing more than fake news to scare people into line--but now... The guardsmen watched him pass, their gazes burning holes through his worn jacket. Just ahead was his townhouse--real brick rather than the facade across town--and he doubled his steps until he was safe. Upstairs, his wife's cough was a creature of pain, cousin to the military man's outside, and John shuddered.

"Illness" by Raven Oak

"The Bell Ringer" by Raven Oak

CHAPTER TWO

On Monday, John's wife tested positive, and he put in for leave at work. It could be hours or days until he caught it, but catch it he would. Each time he trekked to Gerald's, Santa stopped him. The first few times, his words were clear and bright, but as the days passed, his pleas for money were more cough than words, and the sweetness of sick clung to him.

Each trek he hoped the aisles would be stocked, but they never were. Just a few odds and ends, but he grabbed what he could if he thought it might help.

By Friday, his wife's coughing ended with a broken rib. John left his dinner behind as he rushed to the drugstore. When the cane blocked his path, he grabbed it before thinking and gave it a tug.

Santa lost his grip and fell wrists deep into the snow.

"Why are you here? No one's gonna give you money for booze, old man. Now shoo!" yelled John.

Santa fell back against the pharmacy's brick building, hands raised to protect himself.

The pharmacist rushed outside to find John standing over him, his fingers irrationally gripping the man's cane.

Cheeks burning, he dropped the wooden cane. "Tell your drifter here to keep socially distanced. He's gonna make everyone sick."

Before she could reply, John took off down the street at a run. A few slips later, he stood on his porch without the sought-after painkillers and cried.

Christmas Eve arrived with no new snow, though plenty remained on the empty roads.

John trudged to Gerold's Drugs, though this time, he was prepared for the cane. When nothing stopped his progress, John lowered his gloved hand.

Santa lay against the building, money kettle beside him.

Despite the risk, John fumbled his way beneath the man's suit to find no pulse.

The pharmacist stepped outside, her furrowed features softening as John lowered the man's eyelids. "Poor John didn't have many days left in him," she whispered.

They had shared a name, though nothing else as far as John knew. He shrugged. "If you drink too much, it tends to happen faster."

"You know, it was the virus that made him homeless, not booze. He lost his job when his wife got sick and died. Even when he had nothing though, he donated every penny to the homeless shelter on Fifth. He made the nightly trek to give others hope."

John swallowed hard. "I-I didn't know. I thought—"

"You assumed like everyone else. Now if you'll excuse me, I need to call the authorities."

"Wait—cough medicine, do you have it?"

"No." The door slammed shut behind her.

The smell, the hunched over body—for a moment, it wasn't Santa who lay there but John's wife. The virus had reduced the victim to a bag of bones in dirty red, and he saw her, lying in bed in her pajamas decorated by sputum and vomit.

He blinked hard and while his wife's face faded, the thin, sickly body remained, and John's hands trembled as he removed what little cash remained in the kettle.

Fifth wasn't *that* far if he walked fast…

"Empty" by Raven Oak

CHAPTER THREE

John found St. Labre Homeless Shelter wedged between a church and an abandoned YMCA on Fifth and Seneca. When he pulled open the thick, oak door, an old woman wearing a massive, gray sweater blocked his way.

"I was looking for whoever's in charge," he said.

"That would be me now. Sister Villa. How can I help you?"

"I'm here about John? Homeless, dressed like Santa?"

Her smile brightened her brown eyes, erasing years from her face. Somehow, he'd thought her older. These days, maybe they all were.

"Yes! He stays the night here. Brings us money for the poor every chance he gets, kind soul. He should be back anytime now—" She glanced outside at the dark that reached across the city with its skeletal hand, and her smile faltered. "Oh no. Don't tell me…"

"I'm so sorry, but he had this for you." John fumbled with the cash as a cough reached him.

Beyond the doorway, bodies—no, people—huddled together for warmth. Some sick, some recovered, but all of them haunted and needy. All of them alone as no families sheltered here. Not anymore.

John opened his wallet. $400 in cash had been squirreled away in there since the pandemic's start. No one but the desperate took cash anymore. He slid out the four bills and pushed them towards the Sister's hand without a word.

Her smile said it all.

He wasn't the first guilty man to do this, nor would he be the last.

The walk home was long and quiet. Whenever he passed by another soul who ventured out for supplies, he veered far away from them and frowned as they did the same. When was the last time he had given someone a high-five or a hug, other than his wife?

Her face appeared on the missing posters hanging on electrical poles and buildings. As supplies dwindled, some folks disappeared with them. Others entered hospitals, only to leave as dust.

John shook his head. Either he was hallucinating or the pandemic was driving him batty. He skittered up the steps of his building before his mind took another walk.

As he strode past the pileup of dirty dishes and laundry, he heard a light cough from the bedroom. Inside, his wife sat up in bed with a slight smile. "I think I'm feeling a bit better today. My cough feels less…aggressive."

"It sounds like it."

"Oh, while you were out, someone came to visit."

He frowned from the doorway. "Tell me you didn't get up!"

She shook her head and yawned. "He let himself in."

"Who did?"

"Santa Claus. Or he was dressed like him anyway. Said his name was John if you can believe it."

Lightning flashed across John's skin as he glanced around the room in a panic. "Had he visited before? I mean, he was sick, honey. What if he gave you the virus?"

She laughed, and while the action triggered a cough, it was a twinkling sound he'd not heard in weeks. "I've never met him before, but he said he knew you. Wanted me to tell you 'thanks.'"

"Thanks? For what?" He glanced at the wallet in his hands, now empty of money. When he looked up, his wife lay back against her pillows, asleep.

Perhaps she had imaged it. Or maybe he was sick now too. John eyed the home test, then shook his head.

It didn't matter.

He took a scratch of paper from the bedside nightstand and scribbled down the name of the homeless shelter. Perhaps if his wife got better, they'd have a bell he could borrow…

ABOUT THE BELL RINGER

If it isn't obvious, the pandemic has been a difficult time for people like me—disabled, high-risk, immunocompromised folks who understand science enough to know that airborne viruses can be brutal, especially since they mutate.

Before there was a vaccine, let alone boosters, I got COVID from my doctor. Despite the fact that the appointment was the first time I'd left the house in seven months, despite masking and hand-washing, I not only got COVID in 2020, but the virus stuck around in the form of long-COVID. It's the end of 2022 as I'm typing this and the pandemic rages on. I'm still stuck inside, unable to see my friends or attend conventions safely, despite it being a part of my career. Long-COVID left me with debilitating health issues, but I'm lucky. So many have suffered heart attacks, strokes, and worse.

So it shouldn't be a surprise that I wrote a story like *The Bell Ringer*. At a time like this, we need more empathy and compassion in the world.

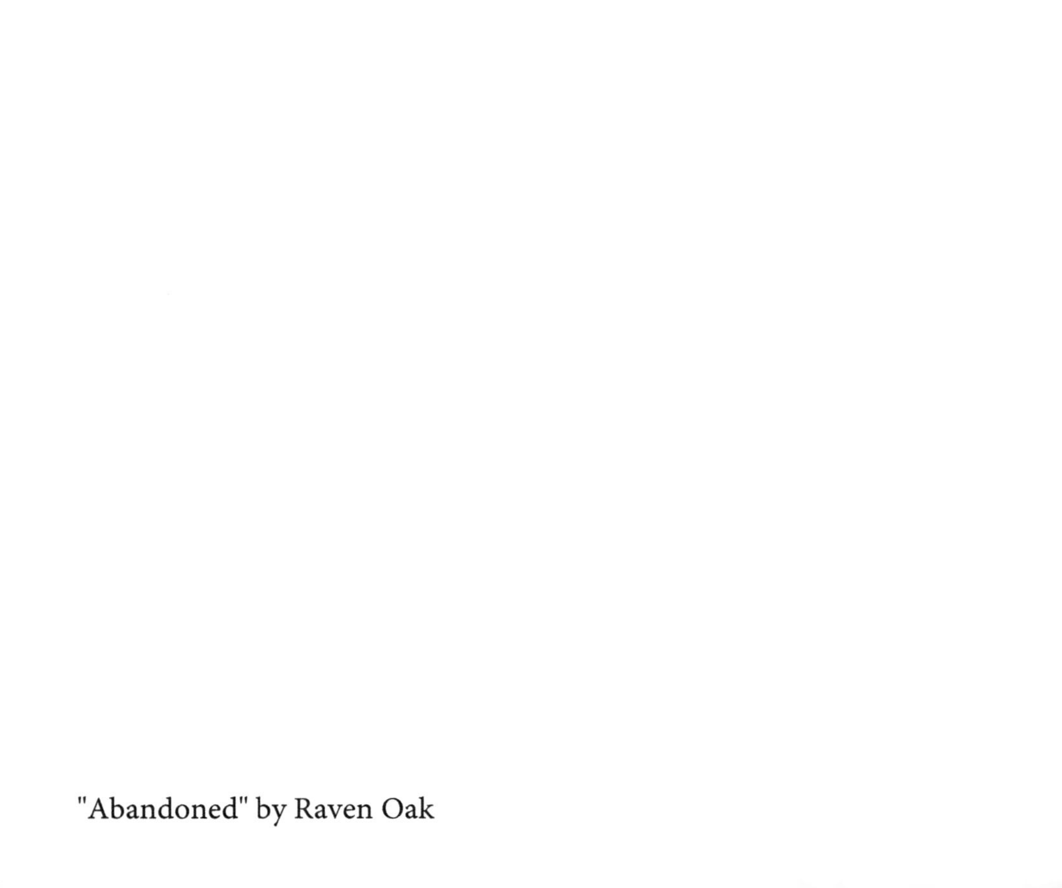

"Abandoned" by Raven Oak

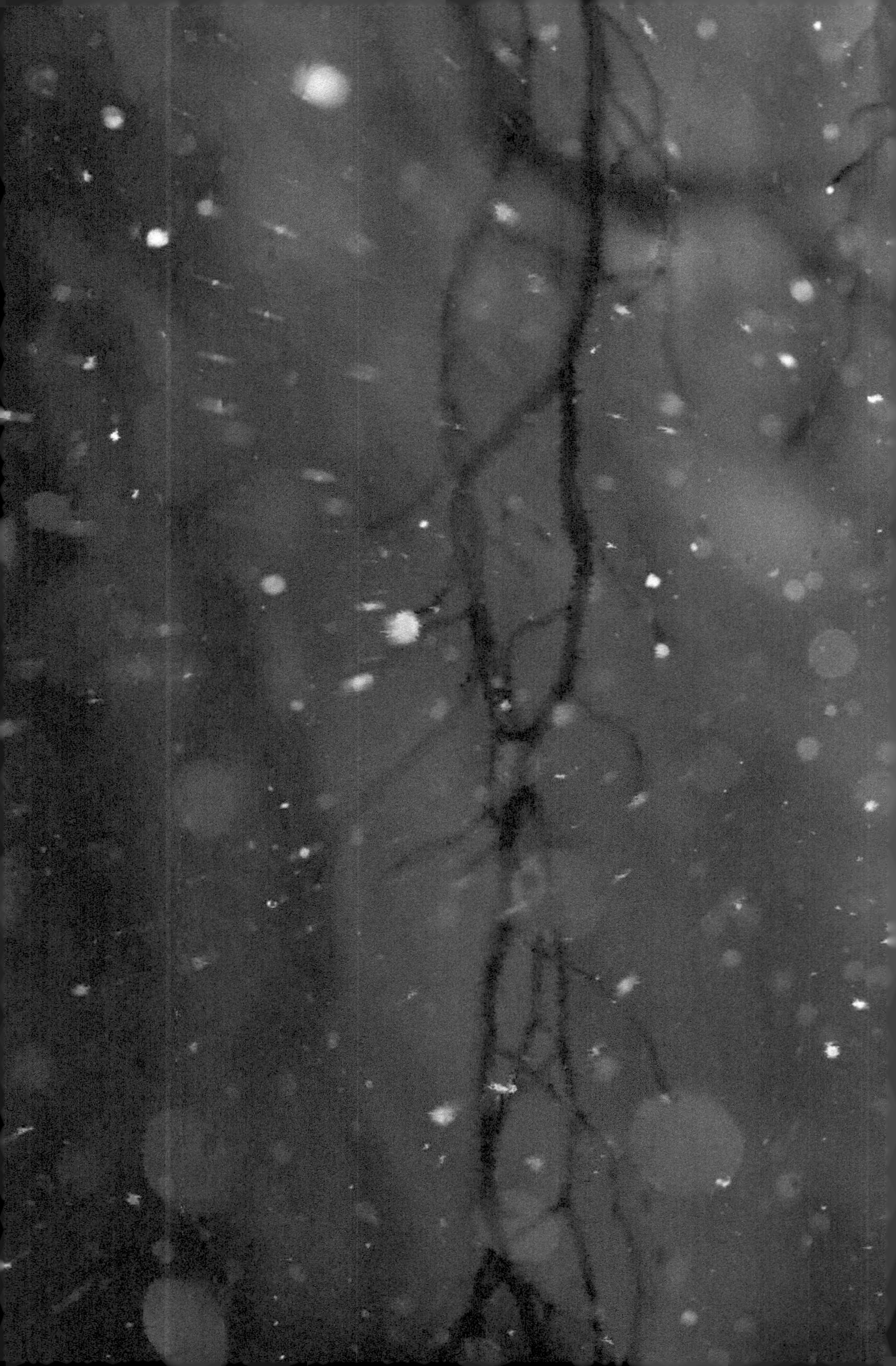

PART II

The Ringers

PROLOGUE

It was an eerie fog if ever there was one.

If fog could envelop every pore of every creature, even then it could not be as dense and adhering as it was that night.

Far outside the grand city of Veleden cowered a village of silence. Whereas you or I might expect sugarplums and mirth in the early days of winter, the village of Dekwcod embraced grays and blacks as evening fell, and its people secured their windows against the creeping fog.

Children buried themselves beneath well-worn quilts, but they didn't clamp their eyes shut. No, they slapped tiny hands over their ears to ward off the jingle-jangle of horses' reins as the Ringers approached.

A guardsman leaned across the jingle-jangle bridle of his perfectly normal-looking horse as it crossed the threshold into town. Snowflakes sprinkled across his red suit and blended in with his white sash. The four men in his brigade, if they could be called men, pulled up alongside him.

Five muzzles puffed frost into the air.

Five men, skin haggard as it draped skeletal frames, sat astride the white beasts.

Five days they would ride and rid Dekwood of those unneeded, those too bold for purpose.

A lone child coughed as he huddled against a tree. Tears mingled with snot as he muᴘ ed his cries with a ragged scarf. ᵗ e bells jangled, the eerie sound carrying through the eve like a death keen. ᵗ e child froze like the snow beneath him, and Ēve faces grinned.

"The Ringers" Original Cover by Raven Oak

1

TWO WEEKS UNTIL WINTER SOLSTICE

The day we sought refuge in Dekwood held no special purpose. Two seasons without work and my papa devised our bold plan. We would load up our belongings in a simple carriage and head north for better fortune.

I was fourteen, convinced I understood everything while understanding very little. It was a dark time to travel, but my mother's womb thickened with my brother and food grew scarce when the grand forests shriveled and died.

How does a forest die? Perhaps it was nothing more than a lack of rain or some magician's grim spell that shriveled the leaves mid-summer and rotted the bark 'til the logs fell without the help of a woodsman's axe. If logging was no longer lucrative, perhaps the more industrialized work of Dekwood could line my papa's pockets.

Five days' travel had left me without purpose. I taxed my mother's patience as I spoke of a spell to change rain into snow or the logic behind the life-giving elements that connected all living creatures and powered the magics of our world. When my feeble attempts to bring about snow froze my mother's morning tea, she hid my magical texts in a locked trunk. Their absence didn't stop me from walking beside the carriage to draw upon the soil's power. Every few hours' travel, I tugged the gloves from my fingers and spread them across the hard earth to feel the thrum of magic beneath me.

And when my mother wasn't watching, I'd whisper the words to call forth a slight dusting of snow across my brow. If she wondered why my red hair bore crystalline flecks, she remained as silent as our days on the road.

On the sixth day of travel, heavy snowflakes tickled my nose. They spread themselves across the hardened dirt road which snaked north to Veleden and south to the City of Escen. I'd never set foot in either, but I'd heard Tellers talk of the great magistrates who managed the towns of the North.

Rumors traveled about the Magistrate of Dekwood, an ageless and grim man who ruled from a hillside mansion. People said he mourned the loss of his sons. Whether from a factory accident or illness, I refrained from asking. Such tales were for *children*.

I was no mere child. I couldn't be if I wished to study magic. One day I would be a magician—capable of powerful magics to bring the trees to bloom and the rivers to flow.

And force the clouds to snow.

I opened my mouth to inquire after Dekwood, but my mother's pursed lips left me silent. My feet ached, but watching my mother struggle to maintain her posture on the bumpy trail made me glad to be walking alongside the carriage. Papa grinned down at me from the coachman's seat.

No manor homes or farms dotted the countryside nor any indication that we grew closer to our destination. I wrinkled my nose when a snowflake graced it, and my mother sighed. "Elise, if you continue to make such expressions, you'll gain wrinkles before you're wed."

Before my soon-to-be brother, an accident that puzzled the Physics aplenty, my mother had spent her days raveling yarn at the seamstress's shop. Like a skein of yarn, wrinkles twined their way across her forehead, and I grinned. "Yours are what I love best about you."

My brashness earned me another scowl before she busied herself with her knitting.

I tried to follow the air across my mother's belly to hear the whispers of my brother—as the Physics had done when my mother had taken ill—but it was only wind to me, the magic far beyond my abilities.

"Papa," I said, and his wood-warped hands tightened on the reins. "Will Dekwood have a school? Something beyond the elementary standard? Perhaps someone with magical knowledge to prepare me for the entrance exams?"

Firm Ēngers loosened their grip. "Any place that close to the City of Veleden is bound to have something. You'll be back to your preparations in no time."

Day ten brought us over yet another hill. A gritty forest loomed ahead like something out of a nightmare, and I shivered beneath my woolen cloak. "Are we to travel through there?" I asked.

His skin paled as we observed the swaying tree-corpses that cast long shadows across the trail. "Don't tell your mother. Go distract her while we pass."

I peeked in the carriage's window. My mother lay across the crunchy, thin-padded seat, eyes closed and breath slow. Her pale hair was messed against a pillow. "She's sleeping." I glanced at the trees and whispered, "But let's hurry."

ᵗ e whites of his eyes reflected his fear, an odd emotion in a man who scaled great heights for his trade, and I shivered.

"Agreed. Last we need is your mother carrying on about evil curses cast upon our future." My papa laid a superstitious hand upon his heart.

Winter tightened its grip on the dead oak, and their bones shivered. Even barren, the trees' branches stretched across the sky and blotted out all light. Like the shriveled Ēngers of the dead they drooped down and reached for us, stealing our warmth and joy before we were more than a foot into the woods.

Nothing lived in these trees.

No sound besides the muᴘ ed hoof beats in frozen snow. No smell beyond the burn of cold air in the nostrils. Branches snagged along my cloak, and I pulled it tighter across my shoulders.

I held my breath 'til I thought I might burst. When I glanced at the spot beside me, my papa did the same and I laughed. The glee bounced beyond us and reverberated back, amplïÿed and shrill.

"Hush," he whispered.

Every now and again, the marks of a woodsmith scored the narrow tree trunks, and a hollow log lay beside our path, a fallen soldier in the battle of survival. And so we traveled for nigh two candlemarks.

Just as we broke free of the forest, my mother sneezed and startled a shrill cry from my lips. "Control yourself, Elise," she said through the carriage's open front window. "A young lady need not give in to such whimsies."

She met my gaze but her death grip on her shawl relayed how long she had been awake.

Papa tapped my shoulder.

Nestled among the countryside's hills, homes rose from the hard earth, their rooftops covered in winter and chimneys smoking with warmth. A great warehouse marred the image, as did the grim mansion on a hill. Dekwood.

Papa grinned. "Welcome home."

2

THREE DAYS UNTIL THE SOLSTICE

No one greeted us. No children scattered snow in the streets or chased a dog into alley carts. A few faces peered out dirty windows the size of dinner plates before fading into darkness.

At the village's center stood a grotesque statue of a man too tall, with a grin too wide that stretched his mouth past redemption. His horse-like teeth were carved of marble, and his hands held a skein of wool.

"Who's that?" I asked.

"The magistrate maybe?" guessed Papa. "Can't think who else would get a statue made of polished stone."

My mother tapped on the glass. "We've a place to go tonight, don't we?"

"From the magistrate. Said so in his letter."

The horses slowed before a brick monstrosity two stories high with edges of cast iron beams and cobbled bricks and stone. Not a brick out of place, and yet the dingy gray embraced the building and marred its appearance.

My mother alighted from the carriage with Papa's assistance. "What is this place?"

"Welcome to the inn," Papa said. He tied the reins to the post out front with a clove hitch.

"Surely we're not staying *here*, are we? Where will the horses be stabled? And the carriage?" My mother pouted at the imposing building, not at all to her customary taste. Inside, loosely grouped chairs and tables gathered dust. A single patron sat at the bar, completely ignoring us.

The woman behind the counter gave Papa a light smile. "You must be Erol Jankin. We've been wonderin' when you'd get here." She squeezed wide hips through the bar opening and ambled over to us, thick pink skirt ruffles dusting the floor as she moved. "The name's Beatrice."

My mother ignored the woman's offered hand, but Papa seized it with exaggerated enthusiasm. "Thanks for the welcome. Noticed quite an oddity on the trip here—that…forest "

Beatrice gave him a curt nod. "You're welcome to two rooms upstairs 'til you can get somethin' of your own. The carriage and horses outside?"

Papa nodded. "In his letter, the magistrate said he'd board the horses—sell the carriage to cover room and board."

"For you and the missus, maybe, but the rooms're too small for the three of you. You'll need another room."

My mother's mouth popped open. "We'd be indebted to this magistrate."

Beatrice's soot-colored eyes settled on the heap of books in my arms. The woman paled at the infinity symbol on the cover, and said, "Shouldn't be long before something comes available, I wager."

The lone patron excused himself as my mother voiced her complaints. Papa forced a smile as Beatrice handed him two keys. "Ain't a kitchen or anything in the rooms, but there's a restaurant 'cross the way that serves meals. I've got the usual helpin's of meat and potatoes in the evenin'. Bread and cheese in the mornin'. I lock up at midnight. If you aren't inside by then, you'll be locked out."

Papa pocketed both keys, ignoring my outstretched hand. "Thank you."

"Won't I need my key?" I asked, and my mother shushed me.

"Mother, I'm fourteen. If I am old enough to attend the Academe, surely I could be trusted with my key?"

"No, ma'am." Beatrice wagged a plump ÿnger at me. "You listen to your folks. Stay in your rooms at night, no matter what you…hear."

"What would we hear?" I asked.

"Bells."

My mother tugged me toward the stairs.

"Bells?" I asked.

"I'll send Vincent to help you unload your belongin's," said Beatrice, and Papa nodded his thanks.

Three steps from the top, I turned to face my mother. "The bells of the spirits? Is that what she meant?"

My mother pressed a ÿnger to my lips. "Don't make trouble."

When I opened my mouth, Papa shook his head. "Listen to your mother."

I didn't know what shocked me more—that there were spirits in town or that Papa agreed with my mother. Either way, I was determined to remain awake and listen for the bells.

3

TWO DAYS UNTIL THE SOLSTICE

Morning brought a misty rain to Dekwood. We stood in the town square, woolen jackets doing little to keep the chill off our shoulders. Either the bells had never sounded, or I'd fallen asleep.

A little slip of a man rushed over to us. Raindrops dripped off his umbrella and splashed upon my plaits.

"Are you Erol Jankin?" he asked, and Papa nodded. "I'm Magistrate du Leunt's assistant. The magistrate sends his most profound apologies."

"Erol, you said—"

Papa patted my mother's gloved hands, tightly knotted over her thickened waist. "I understand, Mr…?"

"Nicolas Ashton. The magistrate can hardly meet everyone who stumbles into town, no matter how…desperate their letters may appear. I'm sure you understand, Mrs. Jankin." He tipped his hat in my mother's direction.

To my father, he said, "I understand your former occupation was a logger in Devlon. I'm afraid we don't have a need for such work. If you wish to pay back your debt to the magistrate—"

"I was given to believe our carriage would cover our time at the inn," said my mother.

"Your carriage was hardly Ēt to cover your stay for a day, let alone a lengthier time." My mother glared at Papa.

Whatever the magistrate had arranged, our plans had changed. My mother squared her shoulders before she spoke. "t en I'm afraid we must take our leave of Dekwood."

Papa whispered something in her ear. Her face paled before her cheeks flushed like a ripe strawberry.

"As I was saying, men work in the leather mill or out in the Ēelds with the sheep." Mr. Ashton frowned as he noted Papa's lanky Ēgure. "I suppose you'll do with the tanner. Little old for apprenticing but work hard, and you could clear your sizeable debt in perhaps a year's time."

Sizeable? We had slumbered here one evening yet our debt was sizeable? Tuition for the Academe would stretch us beyond our means with my mother's need for society life, but surely a few seasons missed work had not brought us to such dire straits? Papa's hand rested on my shoulder, and I bit my tongue.

"Women and those not able-bodied work in the textile factory. Everyone pulls their share in Dekwood," continued Mr. Ashton.

"I'll admit to never having worked with leather before, but I Ēgure can't be much harder than climbing trees in the nippy winter. Say, I was going to ask the magistrate about schools."

"School?"

"Yes, for Elise. Back in Devlon, she was readying for entrance into the—"

t e man's nose twitched with impatience as he waved a hand at Papa. "She's too old for school here. As long as she's got the basics, she has all she needs. Doesn't take much by way of brains to work in the factory, now does it?"

"t e factory? But sir, I'm to study magic at the—"

Like a striped tomcat of Devlon, the man hissed as he stepped back. "Magic isn't tolerated or needed in Dekwood. You'll be working in the factory or none at all."

"t en I'll take none, sir, as I have studies to attend to." Papa's Ēngers pinched my shoulder, and I winced.

"If you know what's good for you, you'll nip that in the bloom now," Mr. Ashton said to Papa with the wag of his finger. "If you want to stay in Dekwood, these are your options." Papa nodded and Mr. Ashton continued. "Work begins an hour after sunrise. Report to the tanner's at noon, and he'll fill you in on the rest. It's just down the street a few buildings and on the right."

"What about housing?"

His eyes, thin charcoal slits at the bottom of too large a forehead, rested on me, and that grin returned. "You shouldn't be too long in the inn."

He'd made it three steps toward the mansion in the distance when Papa called out, "We'll be in contact if we need something. Thank you, and thank the magistrate."

My mother elbowed him in the ribs. "When were you going to tell me of our debt? Had I realized we'd amassed so much in Devlon—" Her cheeks flushed as she turned her eyes on me. Unusually frizzy hair popped out from beneath her wide-brimmed hat, whose red poinsettias clashed with the rich plum of her scarf. She tucked the escapee behind her ear. "Dally about in the rain if you wish, but I've no purpose in this…mess."

We trailed behind her to the inn. A wide road such as this should have played host to many, yet it remained empty. My mother tugged on the doorknob of the inn's solitary door, but the swollen wood stuck.

Papa gave it a good tug and when it released its grip, my mother had an additional reason to scowl so early in the day. The door banged shut behind her. "She'll find reason enough to smile once our situation's settled," said Papa.

I only half heard him as I studied the rain. Like the town, winter here lacked its usual patterns.

As if he'd followed my thoughts, Papa said, "I suspect everyone's at the leather mill or the textile factory. Odd little town this is."

"Am I to join everyone in the factory?"

He sighed. "You've heard more than you should, but your papa's gone and gotten himself into…a delicate situation. It's just 'til we can afford to send you to the Academe."

I frowned.

Something about this town didn't feel temporary—the way

people's drooping shoulders matched their mouths, the way buildings held a hint of desperation with their creaks and wobbles. ᵗ is town didn't release folks to bigger and better things. It kept them tight within its clutches.

Forever.

A shiver pricked goose pimples along my arms, and something deep within the earth made my nose itch.

"What is it?" Papa asked, and I shook my head.

ᵗ ere was no reason to be suspicious of someone using magic, but after Mr. Ashton's reaction to the word, I tucked away the reminder to investigate further. Something just wasn't right in this town.

The Ringers Original Concept Art by Raven Oak

4

ONE DAY UNTIL THE SOLSTICE

My disappointment with the lack of bells warred with curiosity the next morning. The factory doors towered far above my red head. Moss grew between the doorframe bricks, and rust stained the mortar. When I stepped through the doorway and didn't feel magic's touch at my feet, I sighed. A shove from behind sent me sprawling face-first along the floor's dead planks.

"You're blocking the door. Get a move on." The gruff voice's owner shuffled past me, leaving me a spectacular view of worn boot-heels and a coarse gray cloak. My mother's frizzy hair blocked my view of the factory as she knelt, her hand thrust out to take mine. If my mother had been a magic user, the owner of the worn boots would have needed a new pair. Instead, she helped me to my feet and glared as others passed.

From the disabled who hobbled in with canes clutched in knobbed fingers, to the mother with a baby strapped to her hip, women and children of all ages and sizes filed into the factory.

Large looms stretched nigh the full length of the floor, crammed against each other. Wedged in each corner rose four staircases. Women settled into their weaving with a simple rhythm while the children lined up against the front wall.

"You must be the new ones," said a man with a scruffy beard tucked into the collar of his shirt. My gaze landed on the top of his balding head, and I hid my grin. "You—" He jabbed his finger at me. "Join the other children."

My mother inclined her head, and I trudged over to stand behind a girl shaking rain out of her cloak. The man with the long beard led my mother toward the building's rear, and I shivered in the damp chill. "Who was that?" I asked the girl before me.

"That's the Tackler."

"The what?"

She tilted her head toward the looms. "Looms are in-intra-inter—"

"Intricate?"

"Intricate machines. When they aren't behaving, the Tackler fixes them to work so them on the looms can weave. You're the new one, aren't you?"

A girl older than my fourteen years shushed us as the Tackler approached.

"Good—you've already met Charlene," he said.

The blonde folded her cloak and set it on the floor without response.

I pulled mine tighter about my shoulders. "Yes, sir—" His thin nostrils flared, and I ceased speaking and joined the others in a rigid line that snaked around the interior walls.

We followed him silently—not that it would have mattered much with the looms' racket. The queue stopped beside a woman who pumped a foot treadle as her deft hands spun wool through the loom's grid. The Tackler gestured to a girl at the front of the line. "You turned sixteen yesterday, correct?" The girl who had silenced me earlier nodded. "You'll be working with Rebecca to learn the loom until you've developed the skill to weave on your own."

The girl's cheeks flushed at what obviously was intended to be praise, and I bit my tongue. Nothing about this job piqued my interest. A hundred or so women sat on hard stools in silence as they worked with hand and foot in a loud, drafty room. My mind itched for my books, but I followed along wordlessly as the line resumed its movement toward the rear of the building. The Tackler opened two doors and ushered us into a room the size of our old home in Devlon.

I followed Charlene to two stools against the wall. "I'm Elise."

She nodded and pulled two stiff-bristled brushes from a nearby basket. Charlene handed them to me and asked, "Ever carded wool before?"

"Never in my life."

She raised a brow and shoved a small basket of wool into my lap. Her demonstration with the carders proved thorough, but when I tried my hand at it, the wool caught in the spines of the brush. "You're pulling too hard. Be gentle," she said. She stretched the wool until it formed a uniform swath moving in a single direction. Thirty strokes later, mine remained a mass of fibers moving at odds with each other.

"It takes practice?" I asked. While Charlene shrugged, several children hid laughs behind oily hands.

"My ma says your ma used to sew for fancy ladies in Devlon. Is that true?" asked Charlene, and I nodded. "Then how'd you end up so…unskilled?"

I smiled. "My gran says I was destined for greater things."

It had been a point of contention between my mother and my paternal grandmother—right up until she had passed the year before. My gran had studied magic until she had married at her parents' insistence. It was her wrinkled fingers that had first touched mine to the soil and taught me of power.

The gentle lull of brushing the wool relaxed my shoulders, and my head dipped toward my chest until Charlene kicked my ankle. I jerked my head upright to find a woman old enough to be my grandmother in the doorway. I squirmed beneath her gaze until a few giggles caught her attention. "Remove your cloak," she barked.

"I'll catch a chill. Please, I'm not used to…such conditions."

More giggles, which she silenced with a look. Despite her bony frame, strong fingers tugged at my cloak and forced me to my feet. Both carders clattered against the wood floor. I towered over her and with the hunch in her back, she struggled to look me in the face. I straightened my cloak.

The others stared at their wool with rapt fascination. "You're new, so I'll forgive your insolence today. But tomorrow, I expect better. You aren't well-to-do no more, so don't be expecting no favors. Tomorrow, you'll leave your cloak with the rest."

When the doors closed, Charlene released the breath she'd been holding. "Is that woman normally so cross?" I asked, but she rotated her stool until her back was to me.

To keep myself awake, I sketched incantations in my head and wordlessly recited formulas until my hands were stiff and my stomach threatened to pierce my backbone with hunger. When two o'clock arrived, the other children pulled lunches from their satchels. Their meal was punctuated by brief whispers. My feet were nearly numb after half a day on a wooden stool, and I bent over to touch my hands to the floor before rolling up to a standing position. My hand was on the chilly doorknob when someone touched my shoulder.

"Where're you going?"

A boy stood behind me, a roll of bread between his fingers. "To find my mother," I said.

"Can't." His hand against the door kept it firmly shut.

"But my mother has my meal."

"She'll be working now. Her lunch brief was at one," he said.

"I promise I won't bother her. I just wish to fetch my lunch from her bag."

An old puffy scar beneath his eye twitched. "You'll have to eat later. Can't interrupt the weavers."

"But—"

He pried my fingers from the doorknob and once free, pressed one of them against the puffy scar beneath his right eye. "If you interrupt the work, we all suffer, see?"

I jerked my finger away and returned to my stool, though my stomach grumbled audibly. Charlene handed me a wedge of cheese and some dried apple bits.

"Thank you," I said.

"No, thank you."

I got the feeling she was thanking me for remaining in the room, and I asked, "Is it like this every day?"

"Like what?" she whispered.

"Silent. Dejected."

The boy with the scar pressed his lips together, but otherwise ignored us. "There's too much to do for idle chat," she mumbled as she nibbled on a hunk of bread.

"I've never worked before, but surely you could talk while carding —at least as good as you are."

Someone shuffled by the closed doors. Once the person passed, Charlene asked, "You've never worked?"

"No."

"Then whatcha do before?"

"I went to school."

Scar boy laughed. "We've all been to school. What did you do after that?"

"I'm not referring to the elementary standard. I was studying for entrance into the Academe." When Charlene cocked her head, I added, "The Arcane Academe of Veleden."

Two dozen children edged their stools away from me. Those still seated on the ground drew their feet under themselves. "Don't tell anyone," said Charlene. "Magic isn't allowed here."

"Why?"

The boy with the scar strode over and stopped an inch from my face. Mutton and the hint of apple soured my nose. "If you want to survive, stop drawing attention to yourself. Stop asking questions."

"But questions are how one learns—"

"Not in Dekwood."

This time, when the shuffle returned to the door, it didn't pass. The old woman stepped inside, a brown satchel in her hands. "Your mother made quite the fuss 'bout you gettin' this." She thrust the patchwork bag in my direction.

No one in the room glanced at the old woman, but they were aware of her every movement. Even the seven-year-old in the corner watched from the corner of her eye. I took my meal, but I was no longer hungry. How could I survive this town? How could my parents?

Charlene would accept none of my lunch, not that there was any time. We returned to our labors after little more than three bites. The older children shifted from carding to spinning the wool into long threads on spindles. By the time work ended, my arms and back ached. No one complained, nor did they limp or tremble as I did.

My mother's pale head bobbed in the mass outside the room but quickly disappeared as bodies shuffled toward the drafty building's exit. My shoulders brushed against silent townies, and I'd nearly reached the front door when something tugged on my cloak. I had neared the doorframe when I felt another tug.

"Elise," someone whispered, and rough hands propelled me through the door. The bright sun made my eyes water until Charlene's gray form blocked the setting sun. "Elise, I needed to warn you to be careful."

"What reason would I need to be cautious?"

Charlene bit the edge of her lip. "Stop asking questions."

Before I could pry further, she vanished into the throng of workers. Someone tapped me upon the shoulder—my mother. Her shoulders drooped like decayed flesh. "I used to enjoy weaving." She rubbed her expanding middle and frowned. "I hope your father doesn't mind another round of the restaurant's corned beef."

Dinner bearing the consistency of an eraser didn't rest easy with my mind or my stomach, but my muscles screamed for sustenance and rest. It would have to suffice.

Like toy soldiers we formed a line that marched from the factory into the center of town, and from there, bodies separated to their homes without chatter or smiles. As my mother and I trudged toward the inn that served as our temporary home, snowflakes began to fall.

5

THE SOLSTICE

Papa might have possessed the patience for corned beef, but little else that evening had given him pleasure. My questions about the oddness of such a town had fallen by the wayside, as had my complaints about working in the factory rather than preparing for the Academe. His words were placations for ears too young to comprehend their warning.

My ability to attend the bells that evening had waned as exhaustion had set in. My eyes had closed the moment I had tucked myself beneath the scratchy woolen blanket.

When sleep released me the next morning, the inn retained its usual silence and my parents' room lay empty. On the table rested a scribbled note bearing Papa's scrawl.

If you felt like I did yesterday, I figured you deserved the day off. Use it for study, eh? Your mother will tell the factory you've caught a chill. I'll be at work if you need something. There is some bread and cheese in the breadbox.

The cheese was a touch too sharp and the bread just this side of stale, but they numbed my hunger. Outside, snow coated the cobblestone road and dotted the rooftops white against the gray sky. Tempted as I was to stroll past the factory and stick my tongue out at its closed door, the opportunity for a "holiday" pushed sense into my head. Besides, the crudeness of such a gesture would have set my mother to vapors.

The streets were as devoid of children and merchants as the day we had arrived. The town held its breath as its people worked—though for what purpose, I couldn't see. I tucked myself between two buildings and pressed my hand to the cobble, but the crumbling stone blocked any tingle of magic.

The door to the factory protested as it opened and closed, and I tried to sink into the cobble behind me. Charlene frowned at me from the alleyway's end, and I relaxed.

She said, "I thought you were sick."

"I caught a chill but upon waking, felt the air calling to me. Perhaps it might lend health to my lungs."

"Is that magic talk?" she asked, and I inclined my head. "See, that's the very thing that won't sit well with the magistrate."

"What would I care if the magistrate takes pleasure in my speech?"

She leaned against the building and closed her eyes. For all her youth, her frustration aged her and the eyes she turned on me could have been my mother's. "Take care, Elise. People who don't know their place tend to disappear."

"Disappear how?"

"I shouldn't say, but…it's only fair that you know, being new. Have you heard the bells?"

I shivered. "I tried to listen for them our first evening here, but they never came."

Charlene's eyes widened. "Be glad they never came, Elise. Be glad! What do you know of them?"

"Nothing much. Everyone in Dekwood fears them, which makes little sense. Christmas approaches. We should be ringing the bells to welcome the coming of a new year and the gifts of our health and fortunes. To remember the dead and celebrate the future." Her eyes darted to the road as if she expected something, and I tilted my head. "Charlene, why do you dally with me? Shouldn't you be at the factory?"

"I was sent by the Tackler to search for you."

"For what purpose?"

She glanced a third time at the snow-covered street. "To make sure you were being truthful when it was said you'd taken ill." My snickering carried, and Charlene reached up to clap a hand over my mouth. "Shhh, they'll hear you."

"Who? The factory workers? Drafty though the walls may be, they would hear naught over the looms' thrum."

"No, not the workers. The Ringers."

"Beatrice, the innkeeper, spoke of something unnatural in the bells. I've heard talk of spells that can commune with our ancestors, but never with foul intentions. Are these Ringers spirits then?"

"They aren't living. I don't know what they are."

The alleyway dimmed, and I flattened myself against the wall with Charlene. Our movements hid little as the innkeeper glared at us. "I knew you were up to no good. And Charlene—" She jabbed a finger at the girl, whose bottom lip trembled. "—what would your father say to hear you've been talkin' about things better left unsaid? Do you wish to court trouble this close to Christmas?"

The girl squeezed past the innkeeper. I placed a gloved hand on my hip—a gesture my mother would have abhorred—and nodded in the direction Charlene had darted. "I do not see what business it is of yours what Charlene and I discuss."

"Charlene should be at work in the factory, as should you." The innkeeper stopped my sideways motion with a firm grip on my elbow. "Your family's new here, so you don't understand our town and our ways. But the Ringers aren't nothin' to laugh at, and if you know what's good for you, you'll leave it well enough alone."

She didn't stop me as I brushed by, but my insides quaked. I expected a child to fear the boogieman looming in the shadows, but for an adult to fear one so, lent credence to the idea that it was more than a mere spirit or specter—possibly something magical in origin.

Possibly something more dangerous than I was prepared for.

I could have returned to the factory like the young woman my mother wished I was, but I could not. Magical study drew rule breakers and thinkers—people who wished to make order of magic's chaotic nature. If I were to understand these Ringers, I needed information.

And for that, I was going to need my books.

My library rested soundly inside the worn leather chest in my room. The dull buckle remained latched, though the chest had been pushed away from the door. A basin held fresh water from the innkeeper's visit to my room, which was perhaps when she had discovered my escape.

Papa's employ had provided us a certain level of influence in our previous home of Devlon, though not as much as my mother had wished. Despite our more affluent standing, we were held in little regard by those with true wealth. We had ignored my mother's ostentatious nature while saving up for my first year texts at the Academe. My fingers remained gloved as I removed both books from the chest.

The *Livre de Cantus* held the basic foundation for magical studies, and I set it aside. *The Histoires de Créabet Magia*, though, bore the history of magics and creatures of the known world.

I was convinced the answer lay within its pages, but several hours passed, leaving me with nothing more than a stiff neck and aching shoulders. A two-sentence paragraph on the probable existence of ghosts was the only reference to the undead in the entire tome. Nothing on bells or creatures with bells that caused people to disappear.

Information on the undead required a library— specifically, a library with the books of the grand arcanum. A town this small wouldn't have one...or would it? The first day we had arrived, I had felt the thrum of magic.

Downstairs, the innkeeper's fingers were lost to a pile of yarn and knitting needles. She ignored me until I stood beside her, then she glanced up from her needles with a cocked brow. "Do you need somethin'?" she asked, needles still clicking.

"Does this town have a library?"

The yarn wrapped around her index finger stilled. "Do you need a book to keep you company during your…illness?" I nodded, and she fetched a hardbound book from beneath the bar. "This here's a new mystery. Just finished it last week."

"I was hoping to choose my own reading material—" Her scowl deepened, and I retrieved the book from her waiting hand. "Thank you. But if I finish this and wish to read more, is there a library in town?"

"Not enough folks in town read for a library to be necessary. Ol' Henry does us right enough."

"Ol' Henry?" I asked.

"Local trader. Comes by once a month with whatever he picks up out in the world. A few books, some fabrics and yarns, random bits and things. You make sure that book takes no harm. Cost me a scarf and a good bottle of wine."

If someone possessed the books I needed, they weren't sharing. But then, most of the town kept tight lipped. The needles resumed their clicking as I left the inn. Only one person had opened up to me, and she was at the factory.

The factory's front door loomed like the coming snow, and as I crept through, I waited for the Tackler to pounce. His shiny head never made an appearance, though one elder worker nearby thwacked her knuckles on a loom's wooden frame as she worked. No one glanced up, but they shivered in the cold wind that accompanied me through the entryway. The looms' humming drowned out the closing door's snap and those of my footsteps as I sought the rear carding room.

One left turn too many had me lost.

In front of me stood a woman whose wrinkles carried wrinkles. Rather than throwing a wooden shuttle through the floor to ceiling loom, the woman used a metal rod to weave bright colored wool by hand. She hunched over her weaving, her nose nearly touching the wool, and added tiny starburst patterns to a bright blue sky.

"I'm sorry to interrupt, but…" If she heard me, she made no indication, and I stepped closer to the loom. "I said I'm sorry—"

The old woman set the rod aside and cocked her head. I tried again. "I'm Elise, and I appear to be lost." Her mouth moved with slow, exaggerated movements but without sound. "I don't understand—"

"You'll get nothing out of her," said a rough voice. The boy with the scar stood behind me, a basket full of washed wool in his hands. "So many years in the factory, everyone goes deaf."

"She tried to say something. Or at least I thought she did," I said and followed when he gestured for me to do so.

"She was just mee-mawing at you. You'll need to work here a span longer than a day to understand all that nonsense. Besides, I thought you were sick."

My cheeks grew warm despite the chill of the building. "The illness passed, so I decided to return to work."

His basket full of wool bounced, and he pursed already-too-thin lips together. His expression read, *you'd-have-to-be-insane-to-come-back*, but I shrugged it off.

"I became lost and decided to ask directions. What is mee-mawing?"

"The loomers talk without sound, through lip-reading and miming, though I suspect sometimes they just make it up." We turned right where I had turned left and ten feet later, we stood before the double doors to the carding room.

Charlene dropped her carder when I entered, and one of the older girls behind her said, "I thought you said she's sick."

I ignored the jibe and took my place beside Charlene. While yesterday had proven a quiet affair, the youngest children chattered in the corner while those older and nearing apprenticeship gossiped in whispers. I leaned closer to Charlene. "Is it true there is no library in Dekwood?"

"I think there's one in Magistrate Leunt's mansion. My dad mentioned it once. Why?"

"My books lacked the details on a particular research, but if I could perhaps look it up, that may give me answers. How do you function without a library or proper schooling?"

Charlene glanced up from her wool, but no one paid any attention to us in the hum of conversation. "Magistrate Leunt says there's no need for school beyond the basics. What use would we have for such knowledge working here?"

"But haven't you ever wondered why the sky is blue? Or why the snow only falls in the winter?"

Charlene shrugged, but her eyes lit up like buds on spring trees.

I asked, "Or why the trees outside this town have died?"

Several voices paused, awaiting Charlene's answer. "I…" She glared at the boy with the scar—who shared the same pointed chin and green eyes. Only a sibling could level such a look that flushed her skin, but Charlene was daring and she answered me in a quaverless voice. "I asked my dad once why other towns live with joy and food and warmth while ours shrivels like the forest outside. He wouldn't answer."

Air whistled between clenched teeth, and the boy with the scar crossed the room with a dozen steps. He leaned over and whispered something in Charlene's ear.

"No, Matthew, I won't be quiet," said Charlene. "Elise's right. Why don't we have a school anymore? Why is magic forbidden if it's a gift from the gods?"

She rattled off a litany of questions, but my brain latched onto one in particular. *Magic forbidden? It really was forbidden here?* I'd never encountered such a rule or law, but the idea made sense when added to people's reactions. Lost in thought, I missed the door opening and the hush that draped across the room. Something rough slapped my motionless hand, and I tumbled back into the real world.

"—Asleep again? Why aren't you working?" t   e woman before me lacked an arm, yet her single hand was rough, her Ēngers bearing the same calluses of the other weavers.

She raised her hand to slap mine again, and I shook my head. "My apologies," I muttered as I dragged the carder across the wool in my other hand. The woman nodded, but her narrowed eyes followed me as she paced. For ten minutes the room held its breath and worked, and only when the disfigured woman departed did the group return to a hesitant chatter.

Charlene's breath tickled my ear as she leaned close. "My father has a few books. I…I might be able to get them for you."

"Thanks, but I'm looking for something in particular."

"I know, that's what I mean. I've seen them—they have special covers and—"

I clapped my hands over hers to still them. "Wait, your father owns books on magic? Why would your father have those?"

"You met him the other day at the statue. He works for Magistrate Leunt."

Matthew cast aside his work and returned to Charlene's side. He hauled her up by bony wrists and dragged her into the corner where the youngest children worked. "You'll sit here until you can learn your place," he said and glared at me as he fetched her carders.

My fingers tingled in the cold room. The wooden floor kept me from the earth's soil, but moisture licked the air and brushed my cheek with the echo of magic. Air was trickier—thinner and more temperamental—but I set aside the carders and splayed my fingers across the surface of the air.

At first, my fingers remained chilled as I whispered the word for warmth, but after a few minutes, my fingertips flashed with sudden warmth. Sweat broke out across my forehead and trickled down my chin.

The air rose a degree at most before the energy fizzled. I slumped over, my breath haggard. Children stared and whispered. Across the room, Charlene's mouth hung open.

"Get back to work," snapped Matthew.

He did not look in my direction, but the edges of his shoulders and chin left me trembling. Rather than thanks for a warmer room, the children left me in frigid silence. At day's end, Matthew whisked his sister away before I could inquire further about the books. My mother frowned to see me, but must have noted the tension in my shoulders as we left. The walk home remained as silent as my afternoon had been.

I pled out of another corned beef dinner, instead choosing to curl up with the book the innkeeper had loaned me. My eyelids drooped as I turned the pages of yet another boring text that lacked the magic and adventure of the real world. The light peal of jingling bells reached my ears as the book fell against my nose, but when I opened my eyes, the sound was gone. Morning had come.

"Mount" by Raven Oak

THREE DAYS UNTIL CHRISTMAS

I'd grown accustomed to the hum of the looms and the hiss of their whispers. When they vanished, my ears grew acutely aware of the bitter silence in the factory. Before, villagers had offered brief smiles and nods to each other on their way through the front door. Today, no one made motion to do more than shuffle in and stand. Waiting.

But waiting for what?

My mother squeezed my collarbone too tightly, and I squirmed until I tumbled free to skid to a halt before the Tackler. Whereas he normally tucked his lengthy beard beneath his shirt, it rested atop it this morning. His collar was buttoned too tight against slight jowls as he cleared his throat. "Today serves as a warning to us all," he said as he flicked his gaze in my direction. "Everyone plays a role in Dekwood, and when someone doesn't know their place or steps out of it, they're a danger to our way of life. A danger to us all."

A dozen workers over, a woman stifled her sob. The Tackler sought out the source and finding nothing, continued. "Don't let loose the grieving thoughts that plague you, but instead, put your mind toward the task at hand. Christmas approaches."

The voices that recited his words lacked enthusiasm. "Christmas approaches."

The phrase transformed their faces. Where there had rested sorrow and fear, grim determination lit a fire in their eyes as they departed for their workspaces. My mother shrugged as the masses carried her away from me.

"No trouble today," the Tackler barked at me, and I frowned.

I remained silent until I spotted the empty stool in the carding room. "Where's Charlene?"

Matthew's lip welled with blood where he'd bitten it too hard. I repeated the question, this time while staring directly at him, and the carding brush in his hand snapped in half. "Let it go," he muttered.

"Where is she? And why did the Tackler profess such warnings?"

Like yesterday, they were destined to ignore me. I scooted my stool beside a little one stuffing hunks of wool into a basket. "I don't think we've met. My name is Elise. What's yours?"

"Belinda."

"Don't speak, Belinda. The bells will come." At Matthew's sharp warning, the child wrapped her arms about her legs, her eyes wide.

In the back of my mind, the bells jingled as the moon rose, and I dropped my carding brush. "Matthew, the bells did come. Last night —did they not? Tell me, where is your sister?"

He closed his eyes. "The bells shook the air last night, and the Ringers walked among us. I thought they'd come for you—" he said, stopping to look on me with tearful eyes, "—but they'd come for C-Charlene."

This was my fault. I'd encouraged Charlene to talk against her better judgment, and because of it, she was gone. "I-I'm sorry, I did not mean—"

"Didn't mean what? To talk Charlene into her death? Because of your talk of schools and magics—as if such things were possible in Dekwood—she went home and begged to be sent away. Can you imagine? She asked *our* father to be sent away so she could learn!"

Anger flushed my cheeks. "Matthew, I never intended for your sister to be taken, but asking to learn should not be a crime. Where exactly has she been taken? By whom? What are Ringers?"

"The Ringers ensure the peace and prosperity in this town. They make sure everyone serves their purpose. When they...they—when they take you, you're dead, Elise. Gone."

I did not recall when I stood, much less when I fled that room, but my running ceased when I reached the smallest building near the center of town: a lone house befitting someone who served Magistrate Revoir de Leunt. Its bricks crumbled a little less, were a little less faded than those around it, and instead of a single-floor dwelling, the house was its own two-story abode. The wailing from inside—a harsh, keening of pain that carried on with few gaps for breath—confirmed my suspicions.

The front step creaked beneath my foot when a shadow moved behind the window, and the same slip of a man from our second day in town leaned out the open doorway to wave an empty fist at me. "Go away! Haven't you done enough to this town?"

"I'm sorry?"

When he laughed, the wailing inside grew louder. "You watch it, girl. They'll be coming for you next!"

His words should have scared me, but the fluttering inside my stomach ceased as the earth beneath me hummed. Somewhere out there, someone called on the magics deep within the soil. Someone out there was not as backward thinking as the villagers. Someone out there was educated.

But not Nicolas. For all Charlene's belief that her father owned magical texts, not a single drop of power sang in his blood or whispered in his breath.

To him, I said, "I am quite sure they will seek me out, sir, and when they do, I have questions for them."

"You won't be able to ask."

"Why?" I asked, and the crying inside paused.

"Because when they come, they suck out your soul." He retreated and slammed the door behind him, but not even solid oak could drown out the cries inside.

Death magic. It had to be.

If the Ringers took ownership of people's souls, then for what purpose? Fuel? Something to power the dark magics required for the undead to walk the earth? Who would do such a thing? Who could?

I stared at the shadowed mansion that hovered in the distance. The only person people feared outside the Ringers was the magistrate. He possessed power and money enough to control an entire town. And if the rumors were true, he was ancient and learned—learned enough to make my knowledge of magic a mere thimbleful.

The thought filled me with dread.

No matter what words were uttered, Papa stood firm. "Their ways aren't ours, but we're here now. Keep your head down until we send you to the Academe."

"But Charlene is missing." My mother's chair scraped across the floor as she excused herself, and I asked, "What reason do we have to remain in this town?"

"Just a smidgen longer, Elise."

"Papa—"

He closed his eyes a moment. "We owe the magistrate for putting us up here. To leave would be a mark against us."

"Do we need his favor so much then?"

Papa sighed. "A man like that—he'd keep you from school with only a frown. Don't court trouble. By mid-spring, summer at the latest, we should have the means to leave."

I fled, crossing the hall to my room. He had never been a man of excuses before, any more than my mother had allowed her appearance to falter or her tongue to still. Sleep avoided me as I stared opened eyed at the cracks in the ceiling until long after the hum of my parents' conversation changed to snores. When snowflakes tapped against my room's tiny window, I rubbed the sleeve of my nightshirt against the pane to stare out across the town below.

The street should have been bare this late hour, but diminutive twinkles danced in the air, cast off from the shimmer below. Rather than look away, I gaped as five white horses took form beneath my window. Five muzzles snuffed the falling snowflakes. One shook his head and sent up an eerie peal as the bells on his harness jingled—less a jingle and more like the scream of cold air across one's skin.

These weren't mere horses, and the Five men astride them weren't mere men.

Red coats clung to gray flesh that stretched too taut over skeletal frames, and the mouth that grinned at me tugged at the corners until it might have split the near-translucent skin. This Ringer—his blue eyes ghostly and glowing—bore a sash across his red jacket, decorated with symbols burned black into the fabric.

Even from the inn's second floor, far from the touch of the earth, the thrum of magic in the air seeped into my feet. The bells rattled my ears as the horses stepped forward.

I flung my heavy jacket over my nightshirt and stuffed my socked feet into my boots. I threw open the door. Halfway down the stairs, I recalled the hour and slowed my steps to a creep.

The bolt was thrown over the inn's entrance; I shoved it upright with a grunt.

By the time the bitter chill outside blustered my face and threatened to rip the air from my lungs, the Ringers were gone.

Snow filled in the edges of the hoof prints. I followed them down the main street and around the corner toward the edge of town. In the distance, the forest darkened an already dark night, and I closed my eyes before I stepped across the town's threshold.

If they'd crossed into the forest, I'd never Find them. Something… or someone…whined to my left, and I followed the sound into a partially fenced yard. Tucked back against the trees lay a house made of lean-to boards and half-rotted wooden planks. A sagging roof groaned under the snow's weight and out front stood Five white horses. I hurried my steps.

Inside the house, another whine, then a cry, and the air outside warmed. The snow stopped, and my feet sweated inside my leather boots. Magic. *Dangerous* magic.

I didn't know what kind, but the power of it made my vision

swim. I stepped sideways to avoid the horse droppings. Horse droppings? Where they real beasts then? One of the horses shoved his muzzle into my shoulder blade, and I flinched.

The horses were living creatures. But what about the Ringers themselves?

My hand paused on the curtain that served as the house's front door. When a child screamed, I stumbled over my boots as I pushed my way through thick wool. Five beings who had once been men shimmered in the main room. One stood over a child no older than four, who cowered in his mother's arms. Tears stained the child's reddened cheeks and snot gummed up his nose, but no sound or breath escaped his blue lips.

His mother screamed at the Ringer, and when he touched his knotted hand to her flesh, her lips parted round.

I snapped my eyes shut, and inside my boots the soles of my feet burned.

Outside the air split with a cacophony of jingling bells, and when I pried open my eyes, two corpses lay in the corner, their hands tangled in one another's.

They weren't vanished or disappeared as Charlene had implied.

They were dead.

7

TWO DAYS UNTIL CHRISTMAS

"What did you do?" Papa's voice carried more than a warning with the question, and I winced.

"There was magic; I could feel it! I needed to see what these Ringers were about," I said. My mother tore apart the roll in her hands, leaving little breadcrumbs scattered across the table's edge. Preoccupied with watching her, I failed to see Papa move until his hands seized mine in too tight a grip as he stood beside my chair.

"Don't follow them again. Leave it alone. Promise me now."

"But—"

"Do as you're told!" he snapped, and I tugged my hands away. "I'm-I'm sorry I snapped, Elise, but this is dangerous. This isn't growing a tree in the backyard or blossoming a flower in a vase. It's dangerous magic—the kind that comes with decades of learning and leads to evil beings and death. A-and I can't lose you." His voice caught, and what was left of my mother's bread fell to her plate with a thud.

"I need more time to clear our debt to the magistrate. Please mind me," he begged, and I nodded. After that, neither of my parents ate.

When my mother and I walked to the factory that morning, we

passed the coroner's carriage. A trio of men moved two bodies wrapped in blankets—one child-sized and both bundled with care.

"Is that…?" my mother asked.

"Yes."

She wrapped an arm across my shoulder and squeezed. "Listen to your father, Elise. Please."

Up ahead, Papa spoke to Mr. Ashton. Whatever words Mr. Ashton spoke caused Papa's face to pale.

"We'll be late, Elise."

"I'll catch up," I said to my mother, who placed a hand over her swelling middle as she clambered through the snow without me. Papa furrowed his brows when he spotted me, but I hid in the shadow of the coroner's carriage until Mr. Ashton retreated.

"Why aren't you with your mother?" Papa asked when I ÿnally approached.

"I forgot something. Was that Charlene's father?"

Papa nodded. "We're moving out of the inn in a few days' time. Probably after Christmas. Magistrate Leunt has found us a place."

My stomach sank. "Where?"

"Just at the edge of town. It's in rough shape, little more than a lean-to at the moment, but they're going to repair it for us. Can't have your mother expecting in a place as drafty as that. Now hurry along to work."

If the cold air hadn't made my teeth chatter, the news would have done so. The home that would be ours had belonged to the two victims, and the thought of dwelling in such a place sickened me. Would our taking such a home further indebt us to this magistrate?

Papa watched me until I had turned the corner, but I waited twenty heartbeats—long enough for him to leave— before I returned to the statue at the town's center. There was something about this mysterious magistrate we never glimpsed—this magistrate in charge of a town of fear and death.

Animating the dead wasn't impossible, but it was forbidden for a reason.

I glanced into the statue's face. *Are you behind this?*

The stone eyes blinked.

I tumbled backward to land on my rear in the snow.

"It's how he knows." The voice belonged to a man buried in rags reeking of body odor. He ran a hand through graying, oily hair that hung a few inches past the tips of his ears.

"Who? The magistrate?"

"Who else? The man in control. He watches. He listens. And when you ain't right, the red men come."

"The red men? You mean the Rin—"

The hand he clamped over my mouth soured my stomach; it stank of blood and earth. I wriggled, and he pulled his hands away. "Don' say their name. Gives them power."

"What are they? Are they reanimated corpses or something more?"

He shrugged. "Does it matter? Until Christmas passes, no one is safe."

"I know things, sir. Magics. Basic practice, but I could—"

The man shrank back at the word. The coroner's carriage stopped beside us, and a gentleman in a crisp, black suit approached. "Mr. Henry, come with me. It's time to see to Elizabeth and the boy."

The man's face crumpled at the name, and he allowed himself to be ushered into the carriage and away from the watching eyes of the statue.

The carriage set off in the direction of the mansion. If there were answers to be had, they would be there.

No magician worth his salt worked without a library. No one. It was long past the hour to discover what this magistrate was hiding, though it would have to wait. Another day's work missed would be noticed.

The hours dragged along as I carded wool in silence. Everyone gave me wide berth, and for once I did not mind. Papa spent dinner alternating between peering at me from behind his soup spoon and pausing with his mouth open, though he said nothing at all.

That evening, when I watched behind the frosted glass of my window, the Ringers and their horses materialized directly below me. The shortest one, with green eyes of a color that could melt hearts, peered at me beneath his red cap. When he hooked a finger and beckoned to me, I threw the shutters closed with a snap and fell beneath my covers until the jingling bells faded, and the sun crept over the horizon.

Christmas Eve had begun.

The Ringers Concept Art #2 by Raven Oak

8

CHRISTMAS EVE

I abandoned the inn before the town awoke and sought the lone path to the mansion. While I thought myself alone, red weaved itself against the drift covered trees and cobble. In the light of my oil lantern, I thought the trees painted with blood until the red moved. A person perhaps?

The figure ahead turned his green eyes on me.

He was alone, Ringer though he was, and when he beckoned for me to follow, my boots crunched in the fresh snow as we approached the mansion.

A grand porch of white stone led to wooden doors bearing stained glass depictions of angelic figures. Circular turrets framed the house on either side, topped by clay-tile spires and iron finials. When the Ringer's boot heel touched the first of twelve steps, the stone didn't shift, nor did the snow depress under his weight.

"Wait!" I whispered, but he gestured at the darkened porch. "I know, you want me to follow, but…are you real?"

His deep green irises marked his sorrow, and he inclined his head once. I reached out a trembling hand to touch his coat's fabric, but he leaned away from my grasp. His breath came in little puffs as he pointed again to the front door.

He did not progress beyond the first step, though his muscles strained and tugged as if he wished nothing more than to proceed. A small eight-pointed star was burned into the left side of the door frame, and when I touched it, it burned my thumb through my gloves.

"You can't pass…because whatever ties you to this world is here? In this mansion?"

His direct look intensified the burn that coursed through my thumb. "S-s " He grimaced as his tongue hung from the side of his mouth. "S-s-sa-save."

"Save? Or safe?"

"S-save us. All." The bells called out in the distance, and he clenched his hands at his side. "Save."

His figure wavered before it disappeared, and the snow fell in earnest. The doorknob turned beneath my hand, and the door swung open to an entryway of shadows and silence.

Was I expected? Or had the Ringer opened the door?

I muffled a cough in my sleeve as my dry mouth choked on the dust floating through the air. The steps of a grand staircase were draped in rugs long since faded and crushed. When nothing beyond the dust moved, I released my breath in little puffs that danced before me in the chill.

Melting snow left droplets along the wooden floor as I approached the first door on my right. A seating area, followed by a dining room with a table long enough to fit our family, cousins included. Beyond that lay the kitchens and pantry, a smaller eating area, a second living area, and a music room. My fingers lingered on the grand piano, leaving dust trails across the black and yellowed keys.

My breathing quickened, and the wind creaked through invisible gaps in the walls as I approached the grand staircase. The old rugs muffled most of my footfalls as I ascended to the second floor, and once there, I paused outside a room whose open door left a sliver of light in the hallway.

I nudged the door an inch, and when no one shouted or leapt at me, I opened it to a room clear of dust and loneliness.

The library.

Shelf-lined walls held books with gilded covers and lettering in more languages than I had ever seen. In the center of the room, a single desk rested, its velvet-lined top devoid of stationery or ink. The first bookshelf held histories of one kind or another, and I had almost skipped it when I spotted the eight-pointed star near the top: a heavy volume whose cracked spine read *The Accountes & Affairs of the Famile Revoir du Leunt.*

Once I had coaxed the book from its shelf, I settled into the corner with an unobstructed view of the doorway. Not that there was anywhere to hide, but it might have been possible to tuck myself underneath the desk. I squinted at the cramped handwriting on the first dozen pages. Mostly accounts of births and property acquisition, I skimmed first paragraphs until I spotted the pattern of dots in the top right corner of each page.

16: 05, 06, 07...the counting of years or months? The code was familiar to me from my studies. The halfway point of the book held the date of 1693, so supposing the dots' arrangement meant years I flipped to the last page, which was blank.

Was the magistrate adding to this book? I backtracked until I reached pages bearing a style of loose-flowing handwriting that was lengthy in stroke. The last entry was dated almost a century ago in the year of 1743. Blotch marks sprinkled their way across the yellowed page, and the handwriting shifted as his emotions overwhelmed him:

> *My boys—all dead—Nothing good and pure and wholesome comes from a woman, this one more than most as her wyld and evyl ways brought my young Eli to ruin. There is naught more foolish than a young boy in love, and doubly so when in love with a sorceress.*
>
> *She thrice scoffed him before the town and his brothers rose to his aid, as brothers should. For nigh two hours they battled this sorceress and sought to drive off her evyl spells from this village, but ne'er had they fought with such a foul creature.*
>
> *I came upon their bare bodies in the centre of town, my sons' corpses drained of life and warped by magics far darker than taught by decent sorcerers. And she stood above them,*

her smile as grim as the winter's new sun. I will remember her words until my death.

"Your sons thought to best me, Magistrate Revoir du Leunt. I merely wished to walk alone, but Eli would have none of it. Obsessed he was. An unhealthy and unholy sickness was upon him."

Sorceress she may be, but my family's history she knew not, and I smote her where she stood. The ground reached up and buried her in its gaping jaws, but still my sons were dead. Still their bodies lay tossed like stones across the river top.

Tonight, they will wander the land of the dead no more. Tonight, the earth will return to me what was lost, and this town will harbor sorceresses no longer.

The writing ceased, the following pages blank. Not that it mattered. An event over a century ago involving our magistrate—the same magistrate, if the names were to be believed, had cast his sons into the realm of living dead. The skill required to create such beings…

I slid the book back into place. Three more bookcases held a variety of stories and treatises but nothing continuing the family story. Certainly nothing magical. On the last bookcase, I spied a collection of magical texts. Rather than focus on their concealed titles, I shut my eyes and whispered my fingers across their spines. Power ebbed and flowed from them, but my fingertips did not tingle until my hand rested on a slim book wedged between a behemoth of a text and the edge of the shelf.

There was more than power to this book. There was hatred and envy and sorrow.

A well-worn yet simple cover—nothing to call attention in a grand library such as this—yet when its pages fell open at my touch, spells of death and life were sketched in grand detail. I shoved the book into my pocket, though it was not far enough away from my heart for comfort.

My lantern flickered as its oil burned low, and I crept away and down the stairs. As I tiptoed with aching, cold feet, I spotted a lengthy picture on the wall whose frame hovered an inch or two above the carpeted floor. An ugly beast all claws and teeth gnashed his way toward the edge of the canvas. In the opposite corner, a woman cloaked in red velvet crouched, her hands glowing as she fought the beast. I removed one hand from a glove and touched the painting.

Nothing. No response.

But it had to be here! Wherever his workroom lay, it would be on the ground floor. Somewhere that would touch the soil of the earth and open to the air and water of the sky. I set my lantern on the floor and, gripping the painting by its frame, tilted it. Behind the painting, the wall was missing.

The weight of the painting near tipped me on my side, yet I heaved it from the wall above to expose the open archway. As I leaned it against the wall, I prayed no one would awaken to notice the painting's misplacement. I brought my lantern into a narrow stairwell that smelled heavily of iron. A dozen steps down brought me to a metal door, which was unlocked.

The bottom corner dragged across the floor with a cry, and I winced as I wrenched it open. Nothing moved above or below, and I stepped across the threshold into an almost empty room: four bare walls, one archway walled off, and one wobbly-looking chair in the corner. The lone window near the ceiling confirmed I was in a basement. The perfect sorcerer's workroom.

Yet no sigils decorated the sparse room—not even the eight-pointed star that had burned my thumb.

A shift in weight caused the stairs outside to groan. Someone stood outside. I dragged the chair to the window. Even on my tiptoes, I struggled to push the window up and open as its jambs stuck. Outside, bells jingled and a set of hooves stopped before the window.

The Ringer with the green eyes touched the glass, which dissolved with a gust of snow and wind. I pulled my upper half through the window frame and received a face full of snow. More of the powder wiggled its way into my coat as I shimmied through. My jacket caught on the latch, and I gave it a firm tug before tumbling outside.

Something old and angry mumbled inside the room I'd vacated, and the ground beneath me trembled. With no care for the tracks left behind, I tossed up snow as I bolted toward town. Halfway to the inn, the bells ceased, and the earth shook no more.

My breath struggled in my chest until I crawled into my bed, and even then, my thumb throbbed with warmth.

9

I slumbered long past the rising sun and woke to shoulder shakes. When I opened my eyes, the shaking relented, though my mother sat on the mattress's edge as worry lines traversed her forehead. "What time is it?" I asked.

"Long past when young ladies should still be lying about. It's near noon."

Her words brought me upright in bed, and I cast aside my blankets in a rush. I crawled over the footboard and around my mother. "Why aren't you at work?" I asked as I dug through the bedside chest.

"I was. I came to check on you. You aren't ill again, are you?" She pressed a cool hand against my forehead, which I shrugged aside in order to pull on a pair of stiff pants. My mother scowled but said nothing about my choice of attire. Tufts of wool clung to her shawl, which she pulled closer about slumped shoulders. I glanced one-too-many times at my bed, and my mother crouched with a groan. Her round belly brushed against the mattress as she tucked her hand between it and the wooden frame. She would have liked to have been up to her shoulder in her search, but my soon-to-be brother didn't allow for it. Either way, she rooted around quite unladylike and undignified.

The woman who'd always taken such care with her appearance resembled the rest of the town—shoddy, rumpled, and tired. Her pointed shoes were faded and scuffed, wisps of pale-blonde hair had escaped her bun, and the bottom of her gray skirt was torn. Whatever nonsense the magistrate used to hold this town in disarray had to be stopped.

My mother's hand came back empty, but I held my breath rather than allow the sigh to escape. She reached for my arm to pull herself upright. I frowned, and she waved her hand in the air. "I thought— never mind. I need to get back to the factory."

Her heavy steps lumbered down each stair step and once she had arrived at the bottom, I retrieved the book I'd "borrowed" from the very back corner of the mattress. Simple bound, black leather with only the title etched in silver lettering: *Mort de Vie.*

Cold as it would be outside, I could not be caught reading this. My boots went on first, followed by my heavy wool coat, then a cream-colored scarf that reeked of mothballs, and matching woolen gloves. Lastly, I tucked the small book into my coat pocket and set out for somewhere quiet.

Despite the pallor over Dekwood, the sun glinted off the snow, nearly blinding me as I headed for the edge of town. No one would think to seek me out at the house that eventually would be ours, especially not with repairs set to begin after Christmas.

The heavy curtain was missing from the doorframe, making me glad for my coat's warmth. I avoided the living area where the mother and child had been killed. The sun trickling through a wedge of window cast shadows where they'd lain, and I hurried my steps into the next room. The stove held no warmth, but I drew my own as I noticed a child's letters scribbled across scattered paper on the table. My smile faltered when I studied the page.

The little boy had sketched images of the Ringers.

I leaned on the chair, and when it didn't break, I took my seat and retrieved the book. Its innards lacked the printed text of most books on magic. This one held an older, shakier handwriting. Assuming *The*

Accountes & Affairs of the Famile Revoir du Leunt had been penned by the magistrate and his predecessors, this work was by someone—or *something*—else entirely.

Most of the pages held spells—not just incantations or minor cantrips to light a candle or put a hound to sleep—but spells with real power: the kind I'd never see in school, the kind I wouldn't discover until long after I'd grown gray and crooked after the magic had corrupted me.

One spell cast the soul of another into that of a beast, while another claimed to keep all ills at bay. When I turned the page, I dropped the book on the table where its spine splintered. *Clochen Mort de Noël.*

Death bells.

It was more than the cold that chilled me as I read. The half I comprehended was enough.

> *Upon the evenfall of Solstice, submit ÿve upon the land. In the holy circle of Elshirei, draw forth the innocent and pierce the air with peals of ÿve:*
>
> > *Thy will it be,*
> > *ÿve blind will see.*
> > *A year unmade,*
> > *until the spade,*
> > *doth break this circle*
> > *of Christmas that's made,*
> > *And set the risen free.*

The circle was easy. Every spell tied into the earth, into the land, but to create a circle of blood to honor Elshirei the Betrayed was an unclean deed. To raise the dead—

A hand touched my shoulder, and I screamed.

"Please, I didn't mean to frighten you." Mr. Henry hovered beside me. The rags he wore stank of booze, but he turned alert eyes on me in that moment. "I knew I felt something—"

He pressed a ÿnger to my thumb, and the burning pulsed. "You've been to the house," he said.

I nodded. "How—"

Mr. Henry rolled down the collar of his scarf to display the *viziol* branded into the bluish skin on his neck. The protruding *V*, which rose from the top of two nested triangles left me slack with relief, and he shook his head. "I know that look. You think I'm here to save you, save this town, but I'm not."

"But you are a sorcerer, trained in the arts of high magic and served with protecting…"

Tears welled up as he cast a glance over his shoulder. "I've done my duty to this world and look where it got me. Elizabeth and Peter dead—their souls used to keep that filth alive for another year. When tomorrow passes, I'll be one more among the many and gladly so."

"Please," I said as he turned to pass, "Tell me what this is. I don't understand this spell or how to stop it."

He laughed a rich, belly laugh. "If I can't stop it, what makes you think a mere whip of a girl like you can? You've not even earned entrance to an Academe, much less gained an apprenticeship."

"I-I…may not be able to cease this spell's grip, but I must try, Mr. Henry. Please tell me what this spell means." I pointed at the paragraph in the book and the drawing beside it of the reanimated corpse with dull eyes and bells tied at its belt loops.

"I can't work the magic anymore, not for a long while. Something the magistrate's doing, I suppose."

"Were you sent here to stop him?"

He shook his head. "Not me, but my grandpa. He gave his life failing, as did my pa. That madman stripped the magic out of folks after that, but there's something…something deep down. A rumbling perhaps. I can feel it in the earth." His breath smelled of rot, and I took short breaths through my mouth. "He's losing control of his boys."

Outside, the wind gusted, and the planks rattled around us. Mr. Henry didn't notice the goosebumps that decorated his bare arms.

"His boys?" I asked.

"Them horsemen—the bell ringers. Those are his sons he's brought back."

"The story then, it is true? About the sorceress killing his sons?"

Mr. Henry nodded. "Rumors are that his sons deserved it. Either way, that spell's how he did it. At first, the mighty Magistrate Leunt did the killing. He slaughtered four women in their sleep that morning —all of them sorceresses—and used the blood to draw his circle. Did it at the Solstice's dawn, the day after his boys died. He anointed silver bells—it must be pure silver mind you—with the same blood and spoke the words. It near killed him from what I've heard, but then, he'd already had spells in place to protect against that."

"How…how old is he? The magistrate?"

"Older than this town. Or maybe not old enough. It doesn't matter." I closed the book, and Mr. Henry nodded. "Good, get your folks out of this town and away from this madness."

I slipped the book in my coat pocket. "I am not leaving. I am going to break the spell." His laughter drove icy air into my resolve, but I stood straight. "A Ringer asked me to try, so I must."

"Now I know you're nothing but silly. The Ringers can't speak."

"But he did—the one with the green eyes—he asked me to save them."

Mr. Henry tilted his head. "Huh. Maybe the magistrate is ready after all. Too many centuries passed him by in his sorrow. Look, if you're determined to do this, it must be tomorrow."

"On Christmas?"

"On the Christmas."

"Why?" I asked.

"The Ringers feed to replenish the circle's seal between Solstice, when they rise, and Christmas, when they sleep. Look again at the spell."

I retrieved the book and turned to the proper page. Mr. Henry pointed to tiny scribblings near the edge of the page. "The blood cord protect for five full days," I read, then shook my head. "I don't understand."

"To renew the seal, he must remove his protections."

"…And the circle will be vulnerable!"

He nodded. "But you still have to get to it. He'll see you coming. He has his eye on you yet, I'd wager."

"I'm counting on it."

"Mother?"

She laid aside her knitting and waited. How she found the energy after a long day working the factory loom was beyond my comprehension, but every evening since we had arrived, she prepared for my brother's birth. "Hmmm?"

"I need you and Papa to do me a favor." Papa, who'd been stretched out across the bed, sat up, eyes open, and I swallowed hard. "In the morning, I need you to gather the folks in town at the statue. Get everyone to bring all the bells they can—silver bells—"

"Is this about those funny fellas in the red coats? Didn't I tell you to stay away from that evilness?"

My toes curled in my stockings at Papa's questions. "How'd you know about their red coats?"

"Saw them just last night."

"If you see them again, flee. They are killers."

"That's what Frederick at work said. I know I told you to keep your head down, but something wasn't right with how they looked. I couldn't get warm after seeing them." He stared at his knees.

"They are the magistrate's sons, Papa. They died over a hundred years ago, but he brought them back from beyond. He uses the town to keep them alive." The entire story poured forth and by the time I'd finished, my mother was tossing her belongings into a chest. "What are you doing?" I asked.

"Packing. We're not staying here," she muttered.

"That's not a bad idea. Papa, you two should leave. At least until Christmas passes."

"And what makes you think you aren't coming with us? Debt be damned," he said.

I left their room and crossed into mine where I retrieved the book from its hiding place. When I returned, I closed their door behind me and set it on the table.

"What is that?" Papa asked.

"It is a book on dark magics. Foul spells that call for the murder of innocent people. I found it in the magistrate's house."

My mother hissed, "You trespassed?"

"I had to know what purpose he served in—"

"And now that you do, you'll what? Use that book against him? If he's really as old as you say, you won't touch him with the little tricks you know. Besides, no daughter of mine will commit such…ungodly acts!" Papa had found his feet halfway through the tumble of words, and the door slammed as he left.

My mother's knitting needles remained untouched on the table beside the book. "What will you do…if I gather the townspeople?"

"The Ringers will seek out the statue—imagine, a town full of unwillful people— and when I hear the bells, I will know he is vulnerable. I will break the circle with a single smudge. The spell will be broken."

"Surely it can't be that easy."

"Magic is organic. It comes from the earth and the air, the beings around us, and our will. If you remove any of those components, magic dissipates and returns to its natural state. The circle can't be protected if he means to renew it."

I withheld the mention that I'd be trespassing…again, not to mention the danger of crossing a magical circle, vulnerable or not.

She shook her head, and a gray curl fell across her cheekbone. "I'm not sure I understand it, but if you say you can do this, I believe you. Everyone will be at the statue on Christmas if I have to drag them there at needlepoint."

I snatched the book from the table and turned away so she wouldn't see the tears in my eyes.

10

CHRISTMAS DAY

The crisp morning of Christmas dawned across Dekwood — the one day of the year no one worked. Families would gather to eat and celebrate the coming of a new year, of new opportunities, and new beginnings. Sometime after sunrise, Papa would wake as usual and give thanks to *Wothan* for the sacrifices made in our honor. The town, assuming they followed tradition, would sacrifice five cattle— cows if they had it, though sheep would also honor the All-Father. While children dreamed of the gift giving to come, I crept from my bed and into the pre-dawn's falling snow.

Five horses stood in the field nearby, their bells removed as they pawed through the snow for whatever grasses lay underneath. The magistrate's mansion felt hollow to the touch, but where else would a mourning father be but here with his sons?

He would expect me through the front door—that plan would fail. I backed down the steps until my boots touched soil, then I slid first one foot and then the other from my boots. My stockings came next until I shivered barefooted in the snow.

While my feet froze, my skin hummed with the power beneath me. Around the mansion's side, the basement's window waited as paneless as I had left it. The room stood empty, but the chair had been returned to the corner. I drew a circle in the snow with an ungloved finger and picked up a pinch, which melted in my hands. The water droplets returned to the snow as I whispered.

Inside the room, the chair wobbled.

Sweat broke out across my brow, and I removed my wool hat, which I stuffed into my coat pocket. Nothing could leave the circle, not even to join the pile my boots and stockings made nearby. I dug my fingernails into my palms and focused.

Move the chair. Move the chair.

Still the chair merely wobbled.

The barest hints of sun peeked over the horizon, and I closed my eyes to the distraction. The chair trembled. A light scratching as it then slid an inch and another. I panted as drips of sweat sprinkled to land inside my circle. A thud of wood against stone rang out, and I opened my eyes.

Without breaking the circle, I leaned forward and peered down. The chair rested against the wall a few inches to the left of the window. The power drained from me in a rush, and I broke the circle with my chilled finger.

Despite the ache in my toes, my boots remained outside as I slid feet first through the window. I landed too hard on the chair, which fell over and toppled me on my side. Inside the empty room, I sighed and rubbed my hip where I had landed.

Nothing led to the location of his circle. The floor was cold stone, smooth and polished and completely unyielding to my probe for a power source.

I took out the silver ring in my pocket. It had been a gift from my parents, the single piece of silver to serve as the root. If I wished to study at the Academe, this ring was required to cast the compulsory entry spell. An expensive cost for our family but worth the price.

If I used it now, I might never set foot in the Academe.

Two bodies haunted me, and I whispered. The power inside the ring hummed and warmed my fingers. I allowed the warmth to wash over me, and when I brushed my fingers along the wall, a bell on the other side cried out in pain.

"Open," I whispered, and the silver ring dissolved into vapor. The air around me sizzled, and the stone wall wavered five heartbeats before disappearing to reveal a workroom. The walls remained of gray-slab stone, but the floor was compacted dirt and lacked the typical smells of manure and greenery. I poked a single finger in it and listened.

The soil was dead.

A rut formed the circle, its insides rimmed with fresh blood. At its center lay a single bell. Simple and plain, with no ornamentation and a single dent. The bell's original bloody baptism had long faded. I couldn't cross the circle, not yet. Not if I wished to remain living.

Again a squeak on the steps alerted me to a guest, and I leaned against the wall and breathed while my muscles screamed to flee. My feet burned as someone halted outside the visible doorway.

"It's been far too long since there's been a touch on the soil other than my own."

The voice was rich and deep and reminded me of my late grandfather. Far too kind a voice for someone exercising such atrocities. The man who stepped inside lacked the wrinkles his retreating hairline professed he should have. When he glanced at me, his eyes lacked his voice's humor. They carried the empty framing of winter, cold and dead.

I stepped away from him, careful not to touch the circle. The magistrate followed me, and I edged as close to the circle as I could. When he touched the top of my head, my vision swam. "So like her you are," he whispered. "And like her, you've stolen away Eli."

"Eli?"

"My son. He should ride the town with his brothers, yet he hovers behind to watch you. He always carried a heart sickness within him. Horsewhipped by the mere sight of a woman."

I melted under the layers of clothing: rugged pants tucked into men's boots; a plain, button-up shirt; and a coat hanging past my knees. No curves, nothing pink, and certainly nothing womanly about me. "I'm more likely to be mistaken for a boy than a woman. I've not distracted your son, sir. He wishes to die."

"He's already dead."

"Not completely. The bell ties him to this world. He wishes to rest."

The magistrate stepped across the circle. "Simpering fool was always the weak one. Maybe it's time to replace him." He reached for the bell.

"Wait!" I shouted, and his gnarled hand stopped mid-reach. "Why do you keep them animated like this? To serve what purpose?"

"To serve life! My sons were unfairly and untimely ripped from me at the prime of their youth. Why ask such questions though, when you already know this having been in my library."

His thumb smudged a blood droplet as he retrieved the bell. It sounded once, and Eli materialized before us. I scooted closer to the door until my back leaned against a workbench. Now that he was within the circle, I could not break it.

Eli's green eyes glowed in the room's dimness. "Kill me," he whispered, and the magistrate clenched his fist around the bell.

"After all I've done for you and your brothers, you truly beg for death?"

I glanced over my shoulder. A lantern flickered on the table.

While Magistrate Leunt argued with his son, I reached back and grasped the lantern by its base. Its heat burned my fingers for a moment before I tossed it across the circle's threshold. Its glass casing shattered, and the spilled oil caught in a bright flash of flame.

"Dammit," the magistrate muttered and shoved the bell into his pants' pocket. He removed his jacket and used it to beat the flames. Eli swiveled and nodded once in my direction. My thoughts were correct.

Arrogant as the day, the magistrate had failed to protect against non-human physical intrusions.

While he danced with the flames, I smeared my bare foot across the dirt and broke the physical circle. The shock drove the magistrate to his knees as the circle howled, and I retrieved the bell from his pocket.

I had but a minute before he would recover, so I made the only choice available to someone as thoroughly outclassed as I was—I ran.

Boots abandoned, I pounded up the stairs in quite the unladylike fashion. The bell in my hands rang louder than my footfalls, and I burst through the front door as I struggled to listen over the sounds of my haggard breath. Halfway to the statue, I heard them.

Bells.

Hundreds of bells rattling and clanging and jingling as the sun blessed the Christmas day. Behind me, hoof beats on the road approached.

Mr. Henry had clambered up to the statue's arms, where he beckoned for me to hurry.

Between gasps, I shouted at him, "The horse's bells…are ringing! Why…Why haven't they…stopped?"

"We need a circle!" called Mr. Henry.

My feet were nearly numb, but the snow's sting sharpened my focus. There was no time to draw a circle this large. "Quick, make a circle! Shoulder to shoulder, and ring the bells!" I shouted.

Some villagers stopped ringing their bells when they spotted me; none of them made an effort to form a circle beyond my parents, and even they cocked their heads at the request.

The Ringers stopped before the group, and several villagers dropped their bells. A child cried—a whimpering hiccup that awoke the town to the danger before them. Several stepped back while others made motion to leave.

Mr. Henry stopped their flight by clapping his hands together. "Here's your chance. You can fall prey to the Ringers, or you can do what she says. Make a circle and keep ringing those bells! For Elizabeth and Peter and Charlene and countless others we've lost to the bells."

Like a well-manned loom, they circled around the statue with each person's shoulder pressed up against the next as they rang the bells of Christmas. I stood in the middle and called out to Mr. Henry. "Now what?"

"Destroy the bell."

"What? How? The power—"

"Is broken. It's just a bell."

One Ringer reached for the woman in front of him. I held the bell in both hands and snapped its wooden handle. Both pieces tumbled to the ground. Blood coursed off the silver to pool in the snow. The Ringers shrieked—ungodly sounds of torture and joy—yet one set of green eyes found mine. Tears pooled in Eli's eyes as he smiled.

A few villagers paused in their ringing, and Mr. Henry cried out, "Keep ringing those bells."

I fished the bell out from the bloody pool and wiped off the remaining droplets with the corner of my jacket. Once clean, I held the bell by its crown and gave it five chimes.

Five brothers faded from the world. Five sets of bells fell tarnished to the snow below.

And in the distance, a disheveled man rode toward us. I pushed my way through the villagers until I stood as a shield before them.

They filed in behind me, a united wall as the magistrate approached. His years weighed on him like sand; his skin sagged as he dismounted. Each step grayed his hair until it flashed white, and his shoulders curled in on his frame until he hunched over—one lone man before the people of Dekwood.

"Magistrate?" a woman whispered, and he cupped a hand to his ear.

"Say again?"

"Do you know where you are, Magistrate?"

He frowned at her. "No, where am I?" His eyes blinked. When he met my gaze, recognition lit them. He raised a finger in my direction, but Mr. Henry placed himself before me. The *viziol* on his neck pulsed.

"Your magic has returned?" I asked.

He nodded, and the magistrate flinched. Mr. Henry touched his thumb to the old man's forehead. Five counts before the magistrate cackled and tumbled away. His feet carried him to his horse. The effort would cost him, but he mounted swiftly with another cackle. His horse's bells released a sour note as he galloped for the forest of the dead.

"Should we pursue him?" I asked, and Mr. Henry shrugged.

"The spells he used have warped him. Hard to say whether he has any real magic left."

"Good riddance," someone cried, and others muttered similar statements.

My mother draped an arm around my shoulder and pressed her lips to my head. I shivered in the Christmas sun. "Can somebody fetch me some shoes? I seem to have left mine behind."

Laughter draped the village in a glow, and behind me, someone said, "Dearie, you can have whatever you want."

EPILOGUE

Spring brought life to the village. My mother gave birth to my brother, Saul, and the village of Dekwood established Mr. Henry as the town sorcerer. They bestowed the magistrate's mansion on him, though he never set foot inside. Rather than linger with the illness such dark magics cast upon a place, he rebuilt his home at the edge of town and set about restoring the success of its people.

The magistrate never returned to Dekwood.

Some believed he could be heard cackling madly in the forest of the dead, which never grew again, while others said he blew away in the wind that swept over the village in the coming days. Others still told tales of his voice ringing out in the highest pitches of the jingling bells deep in winter.

The bells returned no one, but their jingle held a bitter sweetness for the people of Dekwood until such a time as they forgot the Ringers. When the villagers kept their fear no longer, the forest returned and the looms sang songs of the people's bravery. They smiled to think of the magic that had saved them.

And the red-headed girl behind the magic.

ABOUT THE RINGERS

Originally published in a holiday anthology entitled *Joy to the Worlds: Mysterious Speculative Fiction for the Holidays*, this story is one of my favorites. When I decided to do a holiday collection with a new story, I knew *The Ringers* had to be included.

I can't take all the credit for this story as the baseline idea for it came from my wife. We were driving around Seattle when she said, "What if jingle bells were the bringers of evil? The sound summoned something from our nightmares?" Her questions spun other questions in me. All of our fairytales and mythos have fragments of truth to them. What if Christmas bells did as well?

My brain envisioned undead creatures in red riding white horses through the snow as they traveled to a Victorian town straight out of a Dickens' novel. Once there, they would feed on the souls of the outspoken and the misbehaved. The town knew they were coming by the jingling of bells. Just think of how well the lyrics to *Santa Claus is Coming to Town* ÿt with this picture? And thus, the Ringers were born.

"The Magistrate's House" by Raven Oak

PART III

OL' ST. NICK

Jolly Old Saint Nicholas,
Lean your ear this way;
Don't you tell a single soul
What I'm going to say,
Christmas Eve is coming soon;
Now my dear old man,
Whisper what you'll bring to me;
Tell me if you can.
When the clock is striking twelve,
When I'm fast asleep,
Down the chimney broad and black
With your pack you'll creep;
All the stockings you will ỹnd
Hanging in a row;
Mine will be the shortest one;
You'll be sure to know.

— ORIGINAL LYRICS AS PUBLISHED IN 1881

"Captain Mark" by Raven Oak

Original Cover Art for "Ol' St. Nick" by Raven Oak

CHAPTER ONE

The hole-riddled ship reminded me of my Gran—broken and just a touch too old to remain in an ever-changing world. I'd seen many a battered ship, but standing on the bridge with nothing but a spacesuit between me and possible—scratch that, *probable*—death, set my stomach turning.

Two walls of the bridge were intact, though their computer displays—the undamaged ones, anyway—lay nresponsive. I floated near a hole as tall as me where something had ripped its way through the transport ship's shields and into the hull.

Treaty negotiations between Earth and the New Jhovens left union crews unwilling to contract with freelancers like me. That left my crew and I with salvage work like this. The creepiest kind of work.

Unsettling or not, this job was perfect. Honest theft as these folks had no need of their ship anymore. Besides, we needed the gig. If I had to stomach another protein bar for dinner, I'd be tempted to abandon my *own* damned ship.

Maybe it was *too* perfect. A ship that size, you'd expect someone to miss her or at least miss her crew. If nothing else, word of the attack should have reached someone.

Yet the *Lucky Fish* stood empty—except for my meager crew who floated about scavenging for anything worth selling or using to repair my ship, *The Perffaith*.

Jake's shadow darkened the computer display in front of me. "Fight like this, makes me wonder if there's injured on board."

Half-jx-this, half-carry-that, Jake was my go-to man, though currently he was my *dig-for-parts* man as we combed the *Lucky Fish's* bridge.

"Body scans came up negative for life forms. If anyone's injured, they're long past needing our help, Jake."

"As we boarded, Lissa thought there might be unfriendlies on board. Maybe left over from the fight."

When I turned, his spacesuit's helmet light nailed me directly in the face. I winced, and he tapped a button at his wrist to dim it. "Sorry, Captain," he said.

"If you're that concerned, run another scan."

Jake shook his handheld. "Can't. Scanner's dead again."

No heat sources registered, not even ours, and I swore.

"There are all manner of species that don't read right on our scanners—*provided they work*—so no sense in being lax with security, sir."

I winced at his paraphrasing. "Remind me to give you the job if I ever need a new security officer. You nailed Lissa's deadpan perfectly." Her uptight personality used to be a boon. Now it was just a reminder of our past.

My suit's thick, synthetic fibers protected my fingers from the jagged metal hole in front of me. Jake pulled himself closer until he reached my side, his blond dreads mashed up against his sweaty face. "This is one battle I'm sure glad we missed."

Despite the fresh shave, my black scalp itched as sweat trickled down to my jaw. I glanced at Jake's dreads again.

"Itchy?" he asked.

"Yeah. Must be time to switch out the filters." Yet another thing to add to my growing list of repairs to make whenever we had money again.

"Maybe the *Lucky Fish* will have the parts." Jake's breathing was loud in my helmet's speakers. "I'm glad they ain't here. The stiffs, I mean. Hate when we hafta work around dead folks."

"Open channel two to *The Perffaith*," I spoke into my helmet, which buzzed in response. The channel light flipped to green, connecting me to my chief engineer. "Zac, any luck talking to the computer over here? Or getting her to power up?"

My helmet crackled, and when Zac answered, his voice was louder and clearer than before. "Nope. Something must've blown out the system. I'll need to hop on over to see what's the—"

"Negative, Zac. Remain on board *The Perffaith*." A press of my thumb and index finger closed the channel, and I flipped a power switch on a nearby console. No response. "Gut what you can, Jake. The bridge is a loss. But keep a lookout for the black box."

He removed the protective glass from a panel and set to stripping the innards of anything that didn't show obvious char-marks.

If I could find the black box, maybe I could sort out her last moments… The panel's door below me was fused together. I pushed away from it to float across to a more intact portion of the bridge. One console bore a few scorch marks but little else. The cover almost fell off in my hands, but its insides were a jumble of wires. No box.

"Open channel four." When the light lit, I asked, "Hey, Seb, how's it looking in the cargo hold?"

There was a delay in either the comm or his response. Maybe the *Lucky Fish* was bouncing the signal around. Or maybe our suits sucked. I resisted the urge to rip off my helmet as static squealed in my ears and set them ringing.

"…Salvaged one crate…moved onto—"

"Did you catch any of that, Jake?"

Shoulder deep in computer hardware, he mumbled, "Said something 'bout salvaging a crate."

How helpful.

"Captain, we have an issue." Seb's voice rang too sharp in my ears.

"Report!"

"There is someone unexpected on the ship. A survivor perhaps."

The scanners had gone belly up again. Sweat rolled down my back, and the suit adjusted its humidity levels to compensate. "Where?"

"Unknown, Captain. The heat signature is sporadic."

"Zac—" There was no response on channel two. "Locate Officer Zac Curtis."

A squeal let loose in my helmet and channel five pulsed before autoconnecting. "Captain?"

"Why are you on a suit channel? Hurry up and shut the cargo doors on *The Perffaith*, Zac. I don't need anyone getting any ideas like making off with our ship."

"No-can-do, Captain. I just boarded the *Lucky Fish* to help track our mystery person."

Shit. No one could've survived on this ship full of holes. That left other scrappers. Folks likely to shoot first and ask questions later. At most, I figured we might run across some space critter or another— usually did on a salvage trip—but nothing humanoid or weapon- carrying.

But then, derelicts and wounded ships attracted the most unsavory types, didn't they?

No misplaced shadows lurked outside the bridge. I snatched a serrated hunk of metal debris floating in front of me and shielded myself as I pushed my way along the corridor. Zac, my chief engineer, met me and Jake at the junction between Hallway A and Corridor C.

Zac gripped a piece of a wooden crate. He'd come from the left instead of the right, and I frowned.

Besides being an excellent engineer, the goofy guy had been my best friend since childhood. He must have guessed my thoughts as he said, "I rechecked the cargo hold on my way to you."

The corridor to engineering was as empty as those to the bridge had been. Outside the engine room, Lissa stood guard. The spacesuit hid her muscular frame, but she was imposing enough with the chill across her face.

"Jake, is Seb showing up on the scanner?" I asked. Jake slapped the device. "Is now."

"You and Zac intercept him. I don't want him tracking this heat source alone."

Both men pulled themselves down the corridor. I stuck my head inside the engine room. Two crew members were waist deep in engine parts. Too busy to notice anything but chipsets and circuitry.

I drifted back into the hall to Lissa, "Seen anything or anyone?"

"Nothing yet."

"Stay with the crew members here."

"But—"

I held up my hand and she *tsked,* something she did more often than I liked. Before she could voice her opinion, my speakers squawked. "Captain, we've got a problem."

"What is it, Zac?"

Silence made me hurry—as much as one could in a spacesuit.

More popping and sputtering from my speakers. Zac's voice returned, halting my forward propulsion. "We found Seb. Damned heat source vanished."

"Vanished? Equipment malfunction?"

I'd replaced all the handheld scanners' memory chips last month. Cheap New Jhovensian shit.

"Worse. Our heat source is freshly dead."

CHAPTER TWO

The room Seb had discovered was little more than a closet. Crates and sacks of goods crowded it beyond cozy, and the dead body splayed through the center took up more than his fair share of space. His round belly floated over a thick, black belt cinching pants stained with grease and who knew what else. Then there was the garish red jacket. Ugly thing with too much fur for this century.

"He is freshly deceased, Captain. The body— " Seb's voice cracked, "—still bears warmth."

White whiskers were sprinkled across the dead man's broad chin, and his round cherry cheeks were rounder than I remembered. I forced my hand to relax around the hunk of debris I'd grabbed as a makeshift weapon.

Seb's white skin was near translucent as he hovered in the doorway. He was the only non-human on board, but with a pair of stylin' shades over his eyes and his orange afro wig, you could almost think him human. Right up 'til he opened his mouth and spewed something about the sins of freedom and enterprise in his near-perfect English.

He was the newest member of my crew—the most annoying member of my crew—but right now, I didn't blame him for getting a case of the wiggins.

Petrie, my medical officer, squeezed past him. Her hip brushed his leg, and Seb flinched. "Back away from the body, please," said Petrie. She crouched with a grunt as the crew watched. A sour smell left my tongue too thick in my mouth.

"You good, Cap?" asked Zac.

I blinked several times to clear my head. "Unnecessary complications bug me is all."

"So what happened to him, Doc?"

Petrie glanced at Zac, then returned her attention to the victim. "I'll need to do a full autopsy to be sure, but I suspect he asphyxiated."

"What's the scanner say about that heat source now, Zac? If someone on board killed this man, it's not too far a stretch to think they might kill someone else," I said.

He held up his scanner. The blue grid held a dozen heat sources, every last one of them traceable to the trackers in our suits.

Seb glared at the functioning scanner. "I followed the foreign heat source here before it disappeared. This tells me the man who appeared as an additional heat source is the one lying before us."

"Ya really think someone offed him, Mark? I mean, ship's pretty damaged—what's one more stiff on a ship like this?" Jake asked.

Our dead man lacked a beard the last time I saw him. I blinked away the memory and said, "There's something odd about this whole thing. Between the body, the sensors... This man was alive before we boarded, but how? There's no spacesuit. No air."

"So how'd he breathe? You're right, Cap. Something stinks," said Zac.

"Murder or not, we'll make a full sweep of the *Lucky Fish*." I opened a channel to Lissa. "Get the crew and whatever they salvaged over to *The Perffaith,* then join me in canvassing the *Lucky Fish's* bow. And keep your eyes open."

"Roger that."

"Zac, Seb, search the stern. I'll work from the bridge back."

Both frowned. "I would best seek with you, Captain."

"You're with Zac, Seb."

"But—"

Zac petted Seb on the shoulder. "Don't sweat it. Captain here works best *without* our advice. You'll get used to it."

I flicked Zac on the shoulder, though with my gloves it came out more a tap. I caught his grimace before it disappeared behind his gloved hand.

"I do not understand."

"Give it time. You'll learn to love this ship and its crazy crew once you've been here a while. We rib each other—which means we joke a lot. I know your people aren't so much with the jokes, but you'll adjust," I said. With a nod to Zac, we set out to hunt for a possible survivor…or murderer. Between the debris and bulky spacesuits—I couldn't afford the good stuff—the search was slow going. Other than a few bodies that hadn't been wrenched into space during the fight, no original crewmen remained on the *Lucky Fish.* Our lone heat source was our closeted corpse.

It was a crime worth blowing off, but something nagged me about it. When I returned to the crime scene, a quick search turned up an ID, though I gave it little more than a glance. It was probably fake. Five years and a funny outfit didn't hide those green eyes any more than they hid the scars along his face from one too many brawls.

I dimmed my helmet's visor, blocking out my father's face. It shouldn't have bothered me. We hadn't seen each other in years, and it wasn't like I gave two shits about him. I couldn't afford the distraction. Nevertheless, my jaw ached as I guarded his body. Lissa found me a few minutes later.

"Mark, are you all right?"

"Open channel one—private seal." When the green light inside my helmet flickered, I said to Lissa, "Check out the doorway."

She took a moment to study the frame, stopping near the latch. "The door was pried open."

I pointed at one mark in particular. Paint chips remained embedded in the metal. "Blue paint. *Our* blue paint."

She frowned. "You don't know that for a fact."

"Who else uses Cadmium Blue #20 to label their tools? That's not the normal color used out here. Freelancers Guild uses Cedar Green #8 by and large."

Her gloved fingers flicked a large paint chip from the gouge and sent it drifting into an open bag she held. "It's a common paint color, Captain. For other things at least."

Two channels lit amber in my helmet's display. "Release privacy status," I said and spotted Zac floating toward us with Seb a foot behind.

"Captain, ship's clear as clear can be," said Zac. Seb confirmed the clear status with a nod.

Lissa handed me the key card to the victim's room.

Someone—probably me—was gonna get to dig through his belongings.

"I know I asked before, but are you okay, Mark? You look… shaken," she said.

I turned from that look, a look that wasn't hers to give anymore. Text on the card said Room 5, Level 3. No power meant no lift, so I set out for the emergency stairs. I used the railing to pull myself up until my helmet lamp shined on the number three. When I paused in my ascent, I caught Lissa trailing behind me. "You didn't have to come along."

"You're searching the room."

"Someone has to."

"How do we know it's his room?"

I shrugged. "Not sure, but if nothing else, I'd like to know why he carried the key card."

As we stopped outside room five, I took a deep breath. Like the closet-sized room we'd found him in, the door had been forced open. Pry marks made by something metal had left regular indentations on it. *Unlike* his final resting place, no blue paint chips marred these. I pointed this out to Lissa before we stepped inside.

A fold-up cot filled the majority of the room. Five wall-drawers shared space with a pull-out sink and toilet bowl.

Typical traveler's quarters. I almost laughed to think of someone as flamboyant and crass as Nick living out of a room like this.

I would've figured he'd opt for a suite.

My light reflected off something on the floor, and I rotated upside down to retrieve it. Glass. "Give me a hand," I muttered, and Lissa gave my legs a push 'til I got upright.

"What is it?"

I held it up to our eye level. "Looks like a snow globe. Used to have one of these as a kid." Small, white dust swirled around inside the glass dome and glittered in my light.

She held up an old paperback just as Zac and Seb crossed through the doorway.

"Is that an honest-to-god real book?" asked Zac.

I nodded and set the glass object on the cot. "Real paper, too. I take it your search is done?"

"Yep. Na-da-thing on board but us."

Lissa passed the book to Zac, and he gasped at the cover. "It's our victim!" On the cover, a fat man in a red suit grinned at us. "The Tale of Jolly Ol' Saint Nicholas. Some old artifact from Earth, maybe?"

As much as I hated to admit it, the saint did bear a certain cheesy resemblance to our victim. It was uncanny the way those same green eyes stared back at me, and for a moment, I was a child again and running.

Always running.

"Captain, look." Zac pointed to some text on the front page. "Says here this Saint Nicholas man was some special dignitary on Earth way back when."

There was a cough in my ears. Seb and Jake crowded around the door, hanging on every word Zac uttered as he continued to ramble on about some long dead holiday where folks exchanged gifts and sang about happier times.

"That body isn't a saint. Certainly not some gift-giver," I muttered.

The chatter around me ceased, and Zac cocked his head. "How you figure? Looks like the real deal—the real Santa Claus—to me."

My brain caught up with my mouth. "Too many scars on him. That man's seen too many brawls to be some cheerful saint. I mean, aren't saints supposed to be holy or something?"

Seb asked, "But how would you explain his attire? It is identical to that on the book."

Damn him. The *Alphan* latched onto anything like it was gospel truth. A habit I'd have to break if he wished to remain first mate.

Seb continued, "He even possesses a—what did you call it, Zac? A traditional gift?"

"What gift?"

"The snow globe and book. A find like this might be worth some coin." Zac's eyes glittered in my helmet's light.

"Should we not be worried about how this saint died?" Seb shook the snow globe I'd cast aside earlier, sending white flutters around the tiny city inside.

My stomach threatened to empty itself right there in all that junk. From simple salvage to a crime scene, this job was everything I'd hoped to avoid. Including seeing my father, Nick. Either way, I wasn't gonna be able to walk away without the answer to at least one question: What the hell had Nick been doing on this ship?

CHAPTER THREE

"According to his identification, the victim's name is Nick Johnson."

Banes, not Johnson. My brain corrected the details. Why'd he choose Gran's maiden name for his false persona? I ground my teeth as the crew crowded around the body like voyeurs. Petrie, my chief medical officer, rattled more information from her examination as the infirmary display scrolled with data.

Petrie continued, "Until we're able to access the derelict's computer, we won't be able to ascertain his purpose on the *Lucky Fish*. Maybe he's following the old Earth myth of Santa Claus." Eyes the color of weak tea twinkled, lending beauty to an otherwise plain face. "The team found a sack full of Earth artifacts stowed in a crate in the cargo hold."

Knowing Nick, the goods were probably stolen. I swallowed back bile.

"The identification plate on the crate's side matches that of our victim." Petrie pulled back the sheet to expose Nick's face. The swollen, red skin marred the sterile and clinical white room. Like someone had opened a can of animal innards and maraschino cherries, molded them Nick-shaped, and plopped them down on the table.

Lissa's shoulder muscles strained against her blue shirt as she leaned over the victim. She held back her long red braids with one hand and pointed at a pinprick in his neck with the other. "Is this how he died?" she asked.

Petrie pointed again at the large display panel. Scans of various organs scrolled by with a ton of numbers that meant nothing to me. "His toxicology screens show he suffered anoxia—"

At our blank stares, she added, "He asphyxiated as a result of exposure to carbon monoxide."

"When? Seb said we had a heat signature," I interrupted. "The victim was alive when we hailed the *Lucky Fish* and found their computer unresponsive. He died within ten minutes of our coming aboard, so where'd he get the CO exposure?"

"And what about this injection or pinprick cut?" asked Lissa.

"Coincidental. Something done prior to death."

I ran a finger over the tiny wound. "You sure, Petrie?"

"Yes, Captain. Cause of death is anoxia."

Behind me, Seb and Zac whispered over the death of *Santa Claus.* Speculation bred rumors, and I shushed them. "Can you tell me how he survived without a ship suit? Was there air in that room?"

"In some areas, oxygen was present and cycling after whatever fight left holes in the *Lucky Fish.*" Petrie's eyes narrowed. "You look like you have another question."

"Yeah, which one of us killed him?" You'd have thought I'd sucked the air from our ship the way Seb gasped. "Do the math, Seb."

I couldn't see his eyes behind those enormous sunglasses he wore, nor did his mouth-flap tilt to indicate comprehension. Seb held up his hands. "There is no math to complete. I assume this is another idiom?"

The only non-Earthling on board, and he spoke better English than me. Toss him a saying, and he'd be chewing on it for the next hour. "Think about it. Victim died of...anoxia, but that room itself took no damage. Air was circulating. So how'd he die?"

Zac asked, "Airflow controller ain't on the fritz, is it?"

"Sensors would've picked up the increase throughout the ship."

"Not with all them holes, Captain." Zac frowned. "Wasn't any air to check. It'd all been sucked out."

Lissa leaned against the wall, arms crossed and eyes narrowed. "Airflow controller was one of the salvaged parts. Booted up just fine for Zac's lackey," she said.

Nick had been right. Damned fool had been destined to die in space. Not that he hadn't had it coming. He was an asshole at best and mobster at worst.

"I wonder if it was a safe room. Pretty common on passenger ships, and it would explain why the room had its own circulation system," said Lissa.

"Maybe this Santa felt all dizzy or something from CO buildup. Messed up and took the wrong drugs? Maybe he went and shot himself up with something that later killed him? Something that interacted with CO levels?" Jake asked.

An interesting idea, but I shook my head.

"Captain?"

I wrested my glance from the stiff.

"Mr. Johnson received a dose of adrenaline sometime before death. If it had been fatal, his heart muscles would display signs of stress, of pumping harder," Petrie explained. "His blood work would show the increase of adrenaline or the chemicals found in whatever drug he could've taken, but nothing showed up in my preliminary tests. The dose he received was too small to do much of anything. Certainly not kill him."

I tapped my gold sliver of a wristband. "Bridge." Once connected I asked, "Did our sensors pick up any trace signatures when we approached the *Lucky Fish*? Like someone leaving as we arrived?"

The crew member on duty answered in the negative, then asked, "Would you like me to run a second analysis of the scans to be sure?"

"Yes, and send the report to my inbox." To my officers, I said, "Maybe the injection was a trick. Something to make us look the other way or ignore his death altogether."

My crew stared at each other, taking turns to weigh suspicions and prejudices. It was comical in a way, made more so by the stripes of pungent cinnamon paste under their noses.

The wall display read 21:04. A long day that would only get longer if I was gonna figure out who knocked off Nick. "Zac and Seb, I want a complete report on the airflow controller and any other parts on the *Lucky Fish* that might explain this. Petrie, run your tests, and Lissa, start looking into what crew may or may not have had ties with our victim. We'll meet at 02:00 in the common area."

Five people I trusted stood around a dead myth until Petrie zipped the mesh bag closed. My officers left the room individually—none of them wishing to turn their back on another.

Not that I blamed them.

Alone with the doc, I said, "Petrie-Dish, I don't want to jump to any conclusions, but I think someone from my crew killed him."

With a glance at the emptying hallway, she leaned close to my ear. "Don't tell a single one of them what I'm going to say, but I agree. You were on the *Lucky Fish* for twenty minutes before we found Mr. Johnson. Based on the body's lack of lividity, he was deceased for approximately ten minutes when Seb found him. He died right under our noses."

"The room was sealed until one of us pried it open, Petrie. It had its own air circulation, but someone tinkered with it."

She wrinkled her nose, but not at any smell in the infirmary. "Then we're all suspects at this point. Someone did something to cause the buildup of carbon monoxide. Question is, was it intentional? I'll run more tests."

She slid the metal tray bearing Nick into the wall and closed the door. The unit locked with a beep after she pressed her hand to the frontal display screen. "Captain, don't take this the wrong way, but something odd did show up in my autopsy."

I tilted my head but said nothing.

"I ran a print scan, and this Nick Johnson, he doesn't exist. There is no record on file."

I allowed the breath I'd been holding to seep out in a slow exhale. "He must be a criminal then. Any record of such things?"

"Captain, when I say there's no record, I mean it. He's a ghost." The stringent odor of antiseptics hit me as she lathered her arms up to the elbow. "I'll run DNA, but that will take time."

My insides trembled. "Keep digging," I said and fled the infirmary.

Once in my quarters, I leaned against the door as my body shook.

I wasn't certain why I was hiding Nick's identity; whether it was for his good or my own, I couldn't be sure, but they couldn't know.

They didn't need to know because *I* didn't kill my father.

I dug through a wall-drawer for a tattered box hidden in the back. I wrestled it from beneath a pair of old boots and set it on my desk. At first, I merely stared at it, but as the silence settled around me like his red cloak, I lifted the lid off the memories.

Nick's face stared at me from the digital photo, his cheeks pink from the mountain's snow. What began as a sigh left me curled in a ball like a child.

I didn't love him—hell, I didn't know him—but now I never would.

"Petrie Dish" by
Raven Oak

"He's Dead!" by Raven Oak

CHAPTER FOUR

I hadn't meant to doze.

e report on the *Lucky Fish*'s circulation system confirmed that the air system was fully operational up until the time of death. Someone from my crew had to have tampered with it. After reading this and grinding my teeth at the implications, I'd dozed until something woke me.

A door rattle wasn't normally the type of noise I'd notice, but my sleep had been uneasy and light. Dreams about the day Nick had left, and Gran shouting at him and cursing his name. Seeing her again, even in dreams, left me brittle.

e bleary wall-clock struck midnight, and thumping footfalls paused outside then continued on.

e door panel glowed blue at my approach. "Display heat sources in corridor A," I whispered. One figure moved toward the common area. It wasn't unusual to see folks moving about, but something in my gut told me to follow. e door hissed open as I left my quarters in pursuit.

e creeping figure ahead wore all black and carried a sack tossed over its shoulder. e overhead lights, dimmed for nighttime, cast jagged shadows, and I cursed the lack of foresight that left me weaponless. A door ten feet ahead opened and closed in rapid succession.

When I approached, the door slid open a second time, bathing me in light. Too much light for the common area. Rather than their normal white, the overhead lights twinkled in reds and golds to the rhythm of an odd thump, and I held up a hand to block the glare. "What in all hells—"

"My apologies, Captain. I was testing their luminosity. Allow me to decrease the illumination." Seb's hairless eyebrows danced above heavily darkened lenses the size of my fist. He dropped the bag on the table before he set about adjusting the lights on a handheld control screen.

"Seb, I don't mean you any insult, but what in the world are you doing in here carrying—" I riffled through the bag. "—A bag of socks?"

He slid a sealed box of thumbtacks across the table. "Once I completed my report on the airflow controller, I researched the mythos of Santa Claus. With one of his servants on board, I thought it might help us through our turmoil if we carried on with our own good cheer."

"Good cheer? During a murder? What are you talking about, Seb? That man isn't Santa—"

He shook out the lengthier socks before tacking them to the wall above the baseboard ventilation shaft. "Captain, I am aware of these facts, but we have a murderer among us. That is not something I wish to dwell on. Instead, I will hang these stockings by the chimney with care—"

"Stop." Another sock dangled between his fingers, this one bearing blue and green stripes, and I asked, "Why are you nailing socks to my ship's walls?"

"In the mythos of Earth's Christmas, Earthlings suspended stockings from chimneys in order to summon the great Saint Nicholas. Also, it is possible they protect against dust bunnies. Are dust bunnies a common fear among Earthlings?"

He hung two more socks on the wall, and I shook my head. "You realize he's a myth, right? Santa Claus isn't real. Neither are dust bunnies for that matter."

Seb continued his "decorating" until ten socks hung from the wall —one for each of my crew—though one sock dangled half the length of the others.

"What's with the short one?" I asked.

"Have you ever heard of *gherblins*?" I shook my head. "Sometimes *gherblins* creep onto the ship at night and steal the socks my mother knits. When my socks no longer possess a mate, I stow them in a box to send home."

"So what? You shrank one?"

Seb shook his head. "After we ferried that group from Yabanc last year, someone left the miniature stocking in the cargo bay. I suspect one of their offspring may have mislaid it."

He slung the empty bag across his shoulder. His mouth- ap split, both top lips forming a half-grin. Coupled with his sunglasses and unusually pale skin, it painted a grotesque picture. My skin crawled like I'd walked through a cobweb. "Is there anything else you require, Captain?" Seb asked.

I wanted to tell him, explain why I was bothering with Nick. I mean, he was my first mate. I should've been able to trust him. Instead, I shrugged it off. "I hate complications."

" at is completely understandable." Seb turned away from the door frame as he continued to decorate.

"Someone killed that man, and I gotta ask, Seb, why do this in the middle of the night? Did it ever occur to you that I might've thought you the murderer? Might still?"

His bushy orange wig escaped his hood when he laughed. "Me? Kill Santa? I am not the one experienced in dead bodies."

"Petrie? Why suspect her?"

"Why not? We are all capable of horrible deeds, are we not? Even you, I suspect."

Yes, I am.

He mistook my silence and said, "No offense intended, Captain." As he sauntered from the room, fro first, I remained alone with blinking lights and empty stockings, both of which chased my thoughts in circles. Petrie had been on my ship during the murder, or so I'd thought. Besides, no way a woman like her would know a crook like Nick, much less have a reason to kill him. Or so I thought.

As much as I didn't want to admit it, Petrie *did* have access to all manner of medicines and the knowledge to cover up the crime. It wouldn't be the first time Nick had steered a new crew member my way in order to set me up. It was time to find out what Ol' Nick had been up to in the years since I'd last seen him.

I swore as I trudged back to my quarters. Nothing good would come of this business with Ol' Saint Nick.

But then, nothing ever had.

CHAPTER FIVE

The sector's trace report noted no fewer than five ships in the area before our arrival, but none of them during Nick's murder. Just my ship, *The Perffaith*. Without access to the *Lucky Fish*'s computer, a spacewalk in a black hole would've been easier than tracing Nick's movements. Zac could've helped, being my local computer expert, but at this point, I didn't trust anyone.

Sad truth was, I wanted to trust them all.

e last time I'd seen Nick, he'd been on Europa running "errands" for Junto, the father of Europa's crime family. I pecked at the handheld screen, which glared in the darkness until I swiped a finger down the side to dim it. A search of his name pulled up a list of warrants, arrest records, and bounties. His current address showed up as unknown. Not exactly surprising, especially if he were still working for Junto.

We'd last met in his shack on Europa. Too much condensation and not enough filtration had left the walls a pattern of black and green splotches, and my nose twitched at the memory.   e business card he'd given me that day—*Raymond Royant, Antiquities Dealer*—had a relay code which I now keyed in. Error messages scrolled across the screen.

"No such contact. Would you like to execute a last known trace-run?"

I hit the "no" button and leaned my head against the wall. How do you find a guy who lives off the grid?

A green light blinked on my handheld. "Incoming Call—Unknown Number."

"Accept call," I said. No picture appeared—just an empty, black screen.

"Whosit?" a gruff voice asked.

"Since you called, you tell me. By any chance, is this Raymond—"

"I asked you a question, boy. Whosit?"

I cleared my throat. "Um, this is Mark Banes. If this is Raymond, I met you once with Nick—"

e black screen fizzled a moment until Raymond's grumpy face appeared. If I hadn't known any better, I'd have sworn he'd been wearing that same annel shirt when I'd met him a few years back. Bloodshot eyes glared at me above a week's worth of stubble. He sat cross-legged in some shack whose walls were lined with cardboard, and he smacked his screen when it grew fuzzy. "I get ya. Yer that turd who left yer dad when he's all sick and shit. Rat bastard's who ya are."

I rolled my eyes visibly, even for a bad connection. "Look, I'm not here to argue his merits or lack of them with you. I just wanna know where he is." I knew the answer, but I was hoping that lying would get me a trail of where he'd been.

"Nick left."

"When?"

"I dunno. Do I look like his secretary? Damn bitch was hot, too. Hotter than me." Raymond took a swig from a bottle he'd been storing between his knees. "Yer hair's shorter than that time you visited Nick."

I ran a hand over my brown head. "He still working for Junto?"

Raymond inched but nodded. e screen ickered then went dark, and the dissonant tritone of a disconnect assaulted my ears.

e last time I'd seen my father, he'd given me some song and dance about being terminal. It wasn't the first time I'd heard that line of bull. Nick's one skill was looking out for number one—that was him. Whether he'd owed Junto's boys money or had bought into some get-rich-quick-scheme, he'd come running to Gran and me when he was low on cash. Or booze. Or both.

And I'd run just a little bit further into space and away from him.

I thought I'd run far enough. Seems as though he'd found a way to run to me.

CHAPTER SIX

Nick's death, the reality that he'd had cancer, and my lack of sleep left me with visions of drunken bums dancing in my head like a bad 3D ick while I contemplated calling Junto. I had a good hour before the 02:00 meeting with the crew. With a heavy sigh, I put in the call to the Callisto Space Station.

I'd repeated my request to five lackeys before I reached someone physically stationed on Europa, then to another lackey before reaching the Family proper. "I know you don't wanna tick off your boss, but see, he owes me one," I said to the funny little man on my screen. His mustache—if one could call a pencil-thin line scribbled above one's upper lip an actual mustache—twitched. "Tell him Captain Mark Banes would like to call in a favor."

e screen went a hazy, snowy gray for another minute or two before the man himself appeared. He'd lost a good fifty pounds since I'd last seen him, and his comb-over was more wilt than comb. I grinned like we were old friends. "How's life in the Family, Junto? You're looking good."

He didn't return my smile but wagged a thin finger at me. "Where is he?"

"Where's who?"

Junto leaned so close to his screen that his nose near bumped against it. "Your father, who do ya think? Son-of-a-bitch nicked some priceless antiquities from…a client. He was s'posed to deliver them to me, but he got all chicky. Took off with the goods."

"Nick's anything but a coward." My left eye twitched, and I tried to ignore it.

"There's somethin' you ain't tellin' me. Now I know I owe you a favor, which I'm willing to make good on, but I can't help you if you're lyin' to me."

"Let me guess. This is what he stole." I held up the snow globe.

This time, his nose touched his screen, and I got a shot of more nose hairs than I needed.

"Where is he? Don't make me—"

"He's dead."

Junto's lips tilted up at the corners.

So he already knew that, did he? I continued fishing. "Found him dead on a beat-up ship out here in the Theros cluster. What was Nick doing on the *Lucky Fish*?"

"I assume hidin' from me."

"And it's just a coincidence that I happened upon him?"

Junto leaned away from the screen for a moment of whispering with some shadow in the background before he returned. "Look Mark, I'll tell you what I know, because we're…friends, but after this we're square. I won't owe you shit. Got it?"

It wasn't a fair trade, and the rat bastard knew it. "Fine. Tell me everything."

"Normally Nick made good on his deals, one way or another, but sometimes he gots to thinkin' he could skip the middle man. Took off with that globe-thingy you got, some honest-to-god books—"

I cut him off. "I mean no offense, Junto, but I already know what he took. Get to the bit about him being all corpsified on the *Lucky Fish*."

Junto's eyes narrowed. "My sources say he'd fooled that captain into thinkin' he was more than some two-credit con artist." He waited for me to react, and when I merely shrugged, he asked, "What? No love for *honest* Nick?"

"Say what you want. He *was* a con man. I've got no warm fuzzies for him."

"Raymond's right. You're quite the bastard. I like it!" Junto laughed with his arms wrapped around a much smaller gut. "Once I found his hidin' spot, I sent some of my boys to recover the goods."

"You sure that was all they were there to do?"

"If I wanted Nick dead, there's all manner of folks I coulda sent. I wanted the loot. That's it."

I shook the snow globe before the screen. "I assume the goods are valuable. Why'd your boys leave without them?"

"Fool captain of the *Lucky Fish* believed Nick. Can you imagine? Thought your old man was some freakin' saint or some shit. Captain refused to give me what I was owed, so my boys got…messy. Ship was in pieces when they boarded. Weren't any trace of Nick or the goods."

"You didn't look very hard."

Junto smiled into the screen. "You know everything I do."

He was lying. If he'd wanted the goods, he'd have taken them. Or asked me to fetch them seeing how I was holding them. I wouldn't push a man like Junto too hard—doing so would only result in my death if I were lucky, and the deaths of my entire crew if I were not—but I could certainly play a little.

"Seeing as how you've gone and lost your goods, what's in it for me to return them? I could part—"

Junto severed the connection before I'd finished. While I had the *why* to Nick's appearance on the *Lucky Fish*, it didn't tell me who had killed him or their reasoning. Junto's boys had been long gone by the time Nick had asphyxiated.

I swiped a hand across my screen to lock it. I'd hoped it would be unnecessary, but maybe the search among my crew would yield more answers. At a minimum, we'd start with interviews.

I hoped my crew was in a truthful mood.

"Hole in Time" by Raven Oak

CHAPTER SEVEN

Before I could shadow my eyes from the twinkling lights, Lissa's pile of braids blocked the brightness. "Morning, Captain." She resumed her pacing while she gestured towards the seat awaiting me.

e rest of my crew straddled benches along either side of the table. Bags drooped beneath most eyes, and no one paid any mind to the socks tacked to the back wall.

"It's not even 02:00 yet," I muttered and hooked a stool leg with my foot. When it scraped across the oor, Seb inched and sent a splash of red sludge over his mug's rim. "Everyone's a mite jumpy this early morning."

Lissa cleared her throat. "Not surprising given the circumstances and lack of sleep."

"Fair enough. I did a little digging about our corpse. Seems he had a run in with Junto and the Family."

"Our stiff was a mobster? Cool." Jake threw up his hands at my glare. "Or not cool. Shame on him. Bad Mr. Santa Mobster."

I rapped my knuckles on the table. "Enough. Junto's boys were long gone when we arrived, so they weren't the killers. Someone on *my* ship murdered Sant—I mean, Mr. Johnson. Maybe it was self-defense.

Maybe it was spur of the moment or even an accident. Either way, we got a corpse on our hands and not a whole lotta answers."

"Are we sure it was one of us?" Lissa asked, and I nodded.

"Analysis says we were the only ship within three hours of the *Lucky Fish* at the time of death. Someone on *The Perffaith* killed him. I want everyone interviewed, Lissa. Where they were, what they were doing—report to me by noon."

"   ere is not any need, Captain." When Seb stood, his eyes hiding behind oval frames, my gut played a round of slug-it-out with my esophagus. "I think we know who our killer is."

Many feet shuffled beneath the table. "Considering we don't have much more than a mob connection and an autopsy, I find that surprising, Seb."

Zac whispered, "   e autopsy. It would be easy to—"

"To what? Lie? Break my oath? Is that what you're suggesting?" asked Petrie. Her end of the bench slid sideways as she rose to her feet. When she leaned across the table toward Zac, Lissa's hand on my arm stopped my own forward motion.

"Might as well see what shakes loose.   is has been brewing all morning," Lissa said.

Without so much as a glance in our direction, Seb said, "Peter, I—"

"It's pronounced Pe-tree, not Pe-ter."

"Petrie then. You cannot deny how easy it would be for you to doctor an autopsy. You have access to needles and medicines we do not, and—"

For all her plain looks, Petrie's height made for an imposing figure as she leaned close enough to kiss Seb.   e tips of her shoulder length hair bounced off his chin, and he   ushed to match the blinking red lights. "Why would I risk my career to kill a stranger?"

"It is not my business to say."

"Don't think I don't know, Seb."

She broke eye contact when I knocked my fist on the table. "Enough double-speak. If you know something, either of you, get to it. Otherwise, sit down and shut up. We've got better ways to spend our time."

"Seb's been spying on me. Late at night when he thinks no one's watching," said Petrie, and Seb hissed.

"Why would he do that?" I asked.

Lissa, who had been calm a moment before, paled. Petrie reached out to grip Lissa's shoulder. "Lissa and I are together. A couple. *Alphans* are not known for their tolerance of…well…"

I closed my eyes. Onboard relationships—damned things never ended well. At best they fizzled out, and at worst, they burned a hole through the ship. A picture of the *Lucky Fish*'s bridge came to mind.

Beside me, Lissa was a confident woman who wore her strength physically as well as mentally. My chief medical officer—Petrie-Dish Extraordinaire as I called her—was an old friend but the complete antithesis of Lissa. Petrie embraced her curves like she had middle age, with shy apologies. e idea of Lissa hooking up with someone suffering under insecurities made little sense to me.

But then, nothing about the past twelve hours made any sense.

Petrie bit her lip as she awaited my response.

"As a general rule, I dislike onboard relationships. However, I see no reason for concern here. What Petrie and Lissa do in their spare time is their own business," I said.

Seb's shoulders slumped forward as Petrie turned away from him. If his mouth- ap could've frowned, it would've. Lissa kept herself angled between him and Petrie, and her finger brushed the taser clipped to her belt.

"Lissa will interview folks, then I'll interview her. She'll send me the reports by noon."

"I'd suggest we search rooms as well," said Lissa.

I waved a hand at her. We weren't there—*yet*. ere had to be an easier explanation to this than murder.

"And who gets to interview you, Mark?" asked Zac.

It was Lissa who answered. "I will."

"But what if you two are in cahoots? I hate to suggest it, but if we're all suspects, we're *all* suspects. Besides, you two have a somewhat colorful past."

Zac was right. I hated when he was right. I rubbed my temples and answered, "You can all interview me. Fair?"

"Whatever you say, Captain."

e edge to his voice confused me. I glanced around the table only to be met by furrowed brows and deep frowns. Trouble was brewing like a solar are. Whatever was happening, I was gonna have to deal with it quickly.

CHAPTER EIGHT

The second run of *THE PERFFAITH*'s sensors showed the majority of my crew on the *Lucky Fish* as they should've been, the exceptions being Zac and Petrie. Sensors indicated both had left *The Perffaith* when Seb had spotted the heat source.   at aside, I awaited the rest of the reports with a spinning mind and stomach.

Another blip—this one from Petrie—pinged my inbox before noon. I don't know what I'd expected the medical report to tell me beyond what I already knew—carbon monoxide poisoning, adrenaline injection, blah-blah medical jargon—but her write-up gave an alarmingly accurate portrayal of Nick's life. I reread the last paragraph twice to be sure I'd gotten it right.

> *Liver cirrhosis indicates a heavy drinker. Scarring of the lungs and esophageal tissue indicates heavy tobacco use. No indications of drug use in the blood or tissue. Five cysts, 2 cm. in size, were removed from the lungs, and two 1 cm cysts were removed left of the trachea. Tests revealed these cysts to be malignant in nature. Patient probably suffered from Stage IV lung cancer at the time of death. No evidence*

*of standard or unusual cancer treatment (radiation, stem
cell placement, etc.) was found.*

Damn. My old man hadn't been lying after all. I closed the report
and put in a call to Zac.

He stood beside a pile of scanners, their motherboards spread out
across the table. "Whatcha need, Captain?"

"Meet me in the captain's station in five minutes."

He nodded as I closed the call and left my room. As I walked to
the bridge I passed Jake, who stared at his shoes. No one on the bridge
paid me any mind. Once the door to the captain's station slid shut, I
settled in behind my desk and pulled up my recent research.

"Officer Zac Curtis requests entry," the computer announced a few
moments later.

"Approve."

e door slid open, and Zac stepped inside. "I figured you'd call
me down sooner or later." When I cocked an eyebrow, he added, "I've
done all I can to try and salvage the *Lucky Fish*'s computer, but the
data's too dang damaged—"

"   at's not why I called you here."

I tapped the screen beside me and angled it to give him a better
view.   e picture of Nick and me was old, but it didn't take Zac longer
than an exhale to make the connection.

His mouth fell open, then closed, and then opened again. "I
assume you plan on telling me why you went and took a picture with
Santa?"

I nodded. "You remember a few years back when my old man sent
me a message saying he was dying?"

"Yeah, but—wait, *that* Nick is *this* Nick?" He squinted at the
screen. "Whoa. Last time I saw his raggedy ass we were both still kids
and your Gran was tossing him out for drinking again. When'd he get
so old?"

I closed the image with a shrug. "Years bouncing from place to
place, doing odd jobs for Junto and his boys will age someone quick
enough." I pulled up Petrie's autopsy report. "Petrie says he was dying.
Cancer."

Zac let out a low whistle. "So he wasn't scamming you last time, huh?"

"Apparently not.   ough it doesn't explain who killed him."

"Or why you're keeping this info secret from everyone," said Zac.

"What happened between me and Nick in the past…is personal, and you'll keep this information to yourself for the time being. It'll only make waves, and the last thing we need is more tension."

Zac nodded, but his fingers toyed with the buttons on his shirt. "You know they'll think it's you. Especially if they discover the damage between you two."

I pulled up the last email I'd received from Nick. "I can't help that. It wasn't me—I've got no reason to kill him."

"Except that he abandoned you and your ma, and later your Gran. Hell, left your Gran with quite the debt if I recall.   en he left you with nothing more than a dream of what a dad's s'posed to be. Sounds like a pretty damned good reason to me."

Zac scanned the email on the screen. "You went to see him?" When I nodded, Zac asked, "Why?"

"Curiosity mainly. You know me well enough to know that I wouldn't kill him, no matter how much I hated him.   e others don't. Especially Seb. He's new to the crew and wouldn't understand."

I didn't imagine the scowl on Zac's face, but like a   ickering screen it blinked away a second later. "Why'd you go and pick him up, anyway? Nothing against his people, but it's uncanny the way he looks at us. Like we're dinner."

Another report scrolled across my screen.   is one an addendum from Lissa on which crew had kin ties to the Europan Family. Only one name popped up, an engineer in Zac's department whose great-great-great grandmother married an ex-mobster.   e details blurred before my eyes. "Junto."

"You took on that freak for your first mate for Junto?" Rather than his usual laughter, Zac's nostrils   ared slightly.

"He arranged for some of the more…lucrative jobs to come our way in exchange for my accepting Seb on board as first mate. It's complicated, and we needed the cash. What can you tell me about Jelgins?" I asked.

"Engineer?" Zac rubbed his jaw. "Seems stable enough. Why? Peg him for the murderer or something?"

"Lissa found a tie with the Family—"

"His great-something-or-other, right?" Zac snorted. "He's no more a mobster than I am. Though Seb, you know he's reporting back to Junto."

I closed the report without responding to his comment. "I need you to hack into Nick's email account."

"What email client does he use?"

"M-net."

"Of course. It's free. Shouldn't be too hard."

My best friend tapped a few buttons and once at the client, he clicked the login button and typed a long word into the password ÿeld. One keystroke later, Nick's email scrolled across the screen.

"Easy password."

"That *was* easy. What was it?"

He rolled his eyes at me. "Your full name."

CHAPTER NINE

Zac left me alone with the emails and my thoughts, neither of which were any good.   e man had barely said more than a dozen words to me (when he wasn't asking for money that was), but had used my name for his password. It left me unsettled as I crawled through messages from Junto and his boys.   e majority were little more than an address and a date and time. Damned fool didn't delete anything. Must've driven Junto crazy with all his rules on security and traceability.

    ree screens in had gotten me nowhere. Rather than spin my wheels on mob business, I pulled up a search to compare Nick's account with the names and email addresses of my crew.   e computer made short work of my search, and the name that popped up wasn't the name I'd expected.

Over a dozen messages linked Lissa to my father, the earliest made two years prior.   e first inquired about the murder of Melinda Mathis-Kerric. I made a note to look into it and kept reading. Lissa's emails to my father grew more insistent, first a short inquiry and when Nick revealed his usual non-caring self, she pointed fingers at Junto, the mob, and finally Nick.

e last message asked to meet, and the date lined up with some vacation time Lissa had taken a few months back. Nothing further appeared in the search, and I typed in a request for emails to Junto on the same date. One result appeared.

Received: by 10.93.34.126.43.122
with SSIMTP id 3927be492;
Saturday, February 8, 2106
03:45:21 (-7 Standard Time)
Content-Transfer-Encoding: ProxyBit.

TO: J3984@i.mw.mail.com
FROM: NickyYB@e.mw.mnet
SUB: Melinda

MESSAGE:
Just so we're crystal, I don't plan to tell her nothing about the
    hit. Ain't like she's Family. So get your head out of your ass
    about this. I got it.

My search on Melinda turned up dozens of articles.   e laser gun used and the way her body had been tossed into the black to drift pointed to a mob hit, but police found little to link her to the Family. She'd once dated one of Junto's boys, but when she'd discovered his ties, she'd broken it off.   e obituary had been brief and lacking emotion, and I skimmed through it until I reached the final line:

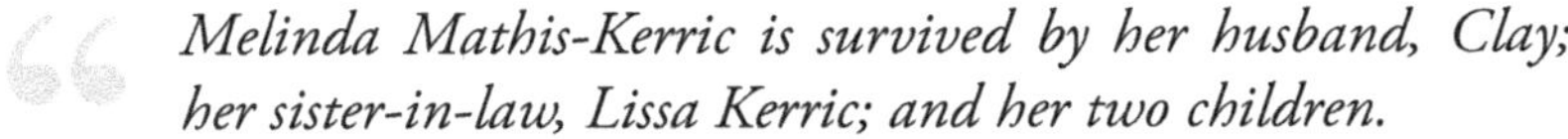

> *Melinda Mathis-Kerric is survived by her husband, Clay;*
> *her sister-in-law, Lissa Kerric; and her two children.*

I tagged the pages and saved them in a folder. Not only did Lissa have the ability to take out someone like Nick, she had motive as well. Dammit, why'd she always have to complicate everything?

When the door slid open to the common area, my crew awaited their turn with a galaxy between each of them. No one talked. No one shared stories about Lissa kicking the ass of some thief or Zac getting *The Perffaith* to limp along on half-baked goods 'til we hit a repair station.   e only people touching were Lissa and Petrie, who held hands under the table.

"I ran a search on everyone's email accounts." Minor reactions to my statement: Lissa's jaw clenched, Zac nodded to himself, and Seb's shoulders slumped. But it was Petrie who surprised me as she bit her lip. "I know where everyone was supposed to be when we searched the *Lucky Fish* and where they said they were, but I want to hear it for myself. We'll start with Jake."

He answered as soon as I finished his name. "Was on the bridge with you, Captain."

"   e entire time?" asked Lissa.

"I followed the Captain to the engine room once Zac let up a shout. Never left the Captain's side."

Zac held up a finger. "Wait, aren't you gonna tell us what you found in your search? I mean, you—"

He stopped when I gave the slight shake of my head. For the moment, the fewer who knew about my crawling into Nick's past the better. Besides, everyone but Lissa had come up clean. She was no Petrie, no jumpy woman who hid behind frumpy clothing and a microscope. Lissa didn't use her physical appearance as some women might either. Her cargo pants weren't too tight, nor was her button-up shirt undone in some lame attempt to sway opinion. Nor did she lean across the table in my direction. Instead, she leveled her gaze on me— relaxation to a T. Had she been this calm when meeting with Nick over her sister-in-law's murder?

"   e data search through user accounts didn't pay off. Nothing beyond the typical came up: porn, family correspondence, the regular. Lissa, retrace your steps for me," I said. A small lie but a necessary one.

"Until Seb spoke of trouble, I was standing guard outside the engine room as requested. No crew left until I escorted them back to *The Perffaith* on your orders."

"You stood outside the doors, not inside?"

"Yes, Captain."

Did you ever leave your post? Did anyone else see you there?

She must've followed along the same thought trail as she shook her head. "No one passed by until you arrived, so no one can verify my whereabouts."

A red light dangling from the ceiling blinked once more before going dark, and my officers glanced up at the sudden light shift.

"Okay, I know this is an important convo and all, but what the hell is all this crap? Besides distracting?" Zac asked as he pointed at the stained child's sock on the wall.

"I had attempted to encourage cheer through the use of items from the mythos of Saint Nicholas," whispered Seb.

Zac held the short sock up by its end. "Yeah, but what's up with the hal ing stocking?"

His laughter pulled up short as Lissa spoke. " at must be yours, Zac. See? It's short like your temper."

Zac's face froze as he clenched his jaw. What used to be jokes between my crew, now caused tension. Something had broken in our group, and a few minutes' laughter wasn't gonna heal it.

 e last thing I needed was a fight, so I returned to the topic at hand. "Zac, why were you coming from the cargo hold when Seb mentioned trouble?"

"I wanted to check on little Seb first. Make sure he wasn't in any trouble, being new and all and most likely to get killed walking up the stairs." Zac slapped Seb on the back.

Seb's sunglasses slid down his nose, and he winced from the lights before shoving the thick glasses back into place.

I would've said he met my gaze, but with his eyes hiding behind his sunglasses, I would've never known. Always hidden—everything about him. He didn't inch or scowl either like I would've at Zac's ribbing. Calm as I'd never been—not since before we'd found Nick's corpse.

"He would not have discovered me in the cargo hold as I was already seeking our heat source. e cargo bay bore an enormous hole in its hull. A single crate remained, anchored to the wall. After the scanners began working, I followed the blip."

"Did anyone see you?" asked Petrie.

He shook his head. "Not until I encountered Jake and Zac."

"And you, Zac?" I asked. "Seems to me I ordered you to remain on board *The Perffaith*."

"Ain't no way I did it. By the time I got on the *Lucky Fish* and got the heat source all sorted out, I would've had no time to reach our vic," said Zac.

I shrugged. "   at leaves you, Petrie-Dish."

"I was on board *The Perffaith* until Seb mentioned the corpse."

"Where on *The Perffaith*?" asked Seb. He was standing again, his mouth- ap curled back and open. "Can anyone confirm your precise location?"

"   e computer can," answered Zac. "   e logs show the correct time stamp for when she left Lissa's room for the *Lucky Fish*."

Interesting. She hadn't been in the infirmary, and Zac had known it. Why'd he been digging through the logs? Seb halted his pacing to glare at Petrie.

Lissa rose when Seb stepped in Petrie's direction—a swift motion I caught out of the corner of my eye. She placed both hands on Seb's shoulders. Lissa towered over Seb and glanced down her nose to see past his shades. "If you've got a problem with Petrie's personal life, get over it. Look at her or anyone else on this ship like that again, and it won't matter that you're first mate. I'll pitch you out the ship myself," she said.

He wriggled in her grasp, but she held him firmly in place. "If you would allow me go."

"Apologize."

Seb shot me a plea for help, and I shrugged. He got himself into this; he could get himself out of it.

"My apologies, Petrie. Everyone." He stumbled back when Lissa released him.

"Captain, I think it's time for that room search. It's too easy for us to cover for one another," said Lissa.

I nodded. Maybe in our search, we'd find something tying someone to Nick, someone else. Maybe I'd figure out what had happened when Lissa had met with him.

Or maybe I'd figure out why it rattled me so much to see her kicking sideways with Petrie.

CHAPTER TEN

Petrie's room was first on our list, if for no other reason than to shut Seb up. Everything tucked into place, her room was nearly unlived in. Dust gathered in the bottom of a laundry hamper and across the food dispenser. Bed neatly made and oor cleared of any tripping hazards. Everything in its place, unused.

She stood, arms across her chest, as Zac and I dug through what few belongings remained in the room. At the door, Seb and Lissa watched, the latter with wide stance as she guarded the doorway.

It didn't feel right to be combing through Petrie's belongings like I was, but my hands busied themselves as my mind wandered.

I almost didn't catch it, so buried was it in a wadded up shirt shoved into an otherwise empty drawer. When my fingers closed around the hard object, I sighed.

"What is it?" Zac whispered, and I opened my palm to display a capped needle.

"Safety ring's missing. I assume it's used, though it's hard to say if it was used on Santa."

In a room the size of a small shuttle, whispers carried like a baby crying. By the look on Petrie's face, she'd heard it all.

" e needle's mine, though it wasn't used on our Santa." Petrie pulled out a vial from another drawer and held it up. "Allergen serum."

"For…?" I asked.

"I'm allergic to Lissa's cat."

Seb muttered something in *Alphan* as he   ed the doorway.

"Run it for DNA…On second thought," I turned and handed the needle to Jake, "have her assistant run it. Send the results to me direct."

Jake left, with Petrie closely behind. Lissa stepped on my boot heels as she followed me toward Seb's room. When I reached the door panel, it read *unlocked* and the room occupied. Lissa stood opposite me, her hand on her taser.

"Be careful, Mark," she whispered, and I arched one eyebrow. "He's been…Petrie wasn't lying when she said he's been following us. Something's off about him."

"Don't tell me you believe all that prejudicial horseshit about *Alphans?*"

"I know you don't want to hear this, but it's true. Seb believes…." She trailed off and stared at the taser in her hands. "He believes that Petrie and I are *taurists*. Evil."

I scanned the band on my wrist to announce us. "You're right, I don't want to hear about your paranoia."   e same old shit as before, only it was Seb this time instead of Zac. Here I'd thought she'd changed in the past few years. "I expect you to do your job without prejudice, Lissa."

 e door slid open with a faint chime. A musty odor itched my nose something fierce as I stepped inside the dark room. Seb's faint shape sat across from the door, his hand shading his exposed eyes from the hallway light. "If you do not mind, please close the door until I have my glasses," he said.

At my nod, Lissa stepped inside and allowed the door to slide shut. We stood in near pitch darkness as Seb rummaged around to my right. A slight hiss closed a metal drawer. When the lights rose, Seb leaned against the wall donning his shades. "Please feel free to search my personal belongings.   ere is nothing here I wish to hide."

As I approached the wall-drawers, my nose   ared at the pungent odor—like sweaty socks in a microwave. No stains along the walls, so he hadn't set any biohazard growing in my ship. e odor was definitely inside a drawer, whatever it was.

I tugged a drawer open at random, and the stench of sweat and something sour bowled over me. Lissa passed me a pair of rubber gloves, and I nodded my thanks.

Nothing hid within the "clean" laundry, but nestled inside the corner desk were three journals, each held together with a sinew-type thread down the middle.

"Please do be careful with those." His voice cracked as he spoke.

"Is that leather? Or…something else?" asked Lissa.

Touching their covers was not in my plan. No telling what skin they came from. Lissa picked one up at random, and I muttered, "I didn't know anyone still wrote on paper. If that's even paper."

Seb bobbed his head up and down. "My mother bound these journals from the hide of a *whonta* on the day of my birth. e inside pages are from the mighty *rew* tree, which stands thirty meters in height. ese books will tell my life story to my offspring and their offspring."

After a few page turns, Lissa handed me a book and pointed.

 **03/1/2108 21:54 PM**

She has remained another evening with the security officer. ey carry on, right under the captain's nose, as if it would not hurt him to see his *amhon* with another. It would crush him.

How could she remain with the security officer? To be *taurists* is unforgiveable, yet she is the moon. How can I see her as such?

Is she unaware that I stood outside for ten minutes? Did I perhaps misjudge her invitation to stop by and discuss current medicinal treatments for the itching of the scalp? Perhaps she meant for me to come by another time. I must have misunderstood. She would not make such an error.

 **03/2/2108 09:20 AM**
I cannot sleep. What am I to do? How can I love something so vile? My mother would be ashamed.

e surveillance dated back months, though his feelings were a more recent development. I snagged the other journals. Looks like I had a little light reading to do tonight.

"Will those be returned?" he asked.

"Once I've taken a look at them."

"Captain," he said, and his shades slid down his nose an inch to expose damp, dark eyes near the size of my fist. "Those—those are personal."

"So was this murder."

My wristband beeped. e DNA results were back on Nick and the needle. I swallowed hard.

"Something up?" Lissa asked.

"Later."

Other than the journals, our search of Seb's room came up empty. e *Alphan* lived an odorous and bizarre life but had nothing connecting him to Nick. Lissa's jaw clenched as we left Seb's room.

"What is it?" I asked.

"I didn't realize...I thought—"

"You thought it was something else, not a crush that had him stalking Petrie."

She nodded. "Not that stalking isn't an issue, but oddly enough, I don't think he's our murderer. He's too much of a chicken shit. ough I suppose he could've planted that needle on Petrie."

"Nope. Tests came back. Only Petrie's DNA on the needle. It was used for her allergy shots."

"Doesn't that mean Petrie's innocent?"

I leaned against the wall with a sigh. "Not necessarily. She could've tampered with her assistant's results or even those of the autopsy. Seb's not wrong on that point."

When she shook her head, the silver beads in her braids glittered in the overhead light. It was good to see her hair long again rather than the short rainfall she'd sported before. "Maybe Seb did a botched frame job? No, it has to be someone else. Why frame someone you love?"

"Maybe because you can't have them?" I asked.   e door panel outside Seb's room changed to the locked signal, and I pulled Lissa away from the door. "I tend to agree with you that he's not our guy, but I can't rule him out just yet. No more than anyone else."

She must have caught the unspoken implication as she pointed in the direction of her quarters. "Let's get this over with."

"Lissa—" I followed her down the corridor. As my security officer, her quarters were next to mine: something that had once been convenient. I bit back my question.

Her room was as I remembered it—simple and without decoration.   e occasional book out of place gave the room a lived in appearance but other than that, her room was as clinical and cold as Petrie's had been.   e exception was the cot, which lay in the corner beneath a mess of tussled blankets. "Tell me, Lissa. Did you kill Santa?"

"No."   e light-brown hand on my forearm was pale against my dark skin. "I thought you knew me better than that, Captain."

"Why Petrie?" I cursed the wrong question that had escaped me. "Never mind, I'm not sure I care to know."

She shrugged and pulled open the wall-drawers for my perusal. I dug through her belongings and swallowed back more emotion than I cared to admit when I encountered one of Petrie's polka-dotted cardigans. "Why'd you meet with our victim, Nick?"

"What?" she asked, her hand in midair. When I didn't reply, she opened her desk drawers, all of which had been locked.

A bit of digging found most of the drawers clear of evidence, and I moved to the single shelf above her cot, which was full of trophies and awards. "You met with Nick concerning the murder of your sister-in-law, Melinda. Why?"

She folded her tall frame into the padded chair in the corner with a long sigh. "Melinda's murder was a mob hit. I knew you had contacts to the Family. I bullied Zac into giving me an email address. He gave me one for a Nick Melorrey. I thought if I talked to him, he'd be able to tell me why Junto called in a hit on her. But I never met with him, not in person."

I was gonna kill Zac for tangling her up with the Family. To Lissa, I said, "   at last job with Junto went way south of normal, Lissa. You almost died. In fact, you left me after that job. What in the world would possess you to get mixed up with the Family?"

"I had to know!"

    e shout caught me off guard, and I shoved a wobbling trophy back onto the shelf. Her cheeks were   ushed and her eyes wide.

"   e police knew it was a hit, but they refused to do anything, Mark.   ey said Junto was untouchable. What would you have done…if it had been me? Would you've let it go?"

No. I would've buried him with my bare hands. "Did you kill Nick?" I asked.

"No. Nick wouldn't tell my anything. He wouldn't meet with me. Just sent me useless emails full of nothing. Hell, I didn't even know our victim was *that* Nick until you mentioned the mob connection earlier."

It would've been easier if I could've believed her. "So you didn't recognize him?"

"I never saw him in person. He wouldn't accept video calls either so no. It seems our victim had many names."

I closed the last of the wall-drawers. "Room's clear."

"You believe me then?"

I spun to find her all too close. She smelled like strawberries, and I leaned forward until my nose nearly touched hers.

"Is this what you came here for, Captain?" she asked, voice colder than the *Lucky Fish*.

I   inched at the door's hiss behind me, and my nose bumped hers.

"Sorry, Captain. Didn't mean to interrupt—" I winced at Zac's words.

Behind him stood the rest of my officers. Petrie bumped into Jake's shoulder when he stopped. "Why the—" Her face crumpled.

"I apologize for suggesting it, Captain, but is it possible you have a conflict of interest?" asked Seb as he brushed past Zac. He opened the wall-drawers with less care than I'd taken. With a shrug, Zac joined him while I stood there looking the idiot. Her room turned up nothing again. Seb stepped back, stray hairs from his wig sticking to his sweaty face.

"Satisfied?" asked Lissa.

Seb stumbled away from her and tripped over a chair leg.

"Since you're convinced there's something going on, we'll do the Captain's quarters next," she said.

ey expected me to lead the way. I'm not sure why I didn't, only that my brain was still arguing with my heart over what the hell had just happened. Zac led the short procession ten feet over with me trailing behind like a guilty party.

Except I wasn't.

My officers watched as Zac and Seb now searched my quarters. I took a moment to stuff Seb's journals into a wall-drawer for later reading.

When Zac and Seb reached my desk, Seb's jaw pulsed. He held up a picture frame I recognized all too well. "Why do you have a photo with Santa?" he asked, and my tongue rolled across the dry roof of my mouth. I'd forgotten to return the photo to the false bottom in the wall-drawer.

e old school digital frame was passed around the crew.

Nick had said he wanted to connect, to make up for lost time while we still had it. Rather than swallow my pride and the past, I'd shut him down. And he'd given up. I might as well have killed him myself.

"Mark?"

Damn Lissa's eyes. If they could've bored black holes through me, they would've.

"I don't know why I didn't see it before." Lissa handed Petrie the wooden frame. "Look at the nose."

"Dominant arch, ared nostrils," Petrie said. "I ran DNA on our victim, Mark. I thought it a mistake, but seeing this picture…"

Zac glanced between the digital photo and me as he shifted his weight from one foot to the other. He tried to hide his *I-told-you-so* expression behind a fake sneeze and failed.

"You knew, didn't you?" Lissa asked, and Zac studied the dirt beneath his fingernails.

I said, "Leave Zac out of this. He was following orders."

"Captain, if you have a connection to the deceased, it would be best to reveal that now." Lissa paled at Petrie's comment.

I took the photo from the doctor. "His name's not Nick Johnson. It's Nick Banes, and he's my father."

Saying the words made them real.

Feet shuffled in the room, but no one spoke. When Lissa's hand touched my shoulder, I inched. "Mark, your father was a first grade asshole. He abandoned you. I think we'd all understand if—"

"If what?" Voice too sharp, I bit my tongue. "If I snapped and killed him? I know what this looks like, but I didn't do it. Much as I would've liked to years back, this murder wasn't me."

"How'd your father end up dead on the *Lucky Fish*?" asked Jake.

"And why were you hiding this photo?" Petrie pointed at the false bottom in the wall-drawer. "No offense, but this isn't looking good for you, Captain."

ere wasn't any way I was walking out of this without being gutted. e story tumbled out too fast, too raw: his scamming first my mother, then Gran; his need for money and booze; the jobs he had done for Junto; and finally, his attempt to reconnect. "He came crawling out of the meteor field to give me some line about dying or some shit. Wanted to get all enlightened with forgiveness at the mountain. at's when that photo was taken."

"And you decided to keep this hidden because?" asked Petrie.

"I wasn't hiding it. It's private and not relevant."

"Not relevant, my ass." Zac ushed. "Forgive me, Captain, but that's what we'd call a motive right there."

Swallowing proved difficult, yet I managed.

Petrie said, "But our victim *was* sick. e autopsy determined that."

"He was, but by the time he'd reached out to me, he'd told so many lies, killed so many…it didn't matter if he was being truthful. Either way, I didn't kill him. Jake was with me during the time of death. Are we done here?"

Zac nodded to Lissa, who announced, "Room's clean."

"Jake could be protecting you, Captain. It wouldn't be the first time someone from your crew kept you from the noose.   at last job from Junto…." said Zac, and I could've strangled him. Zac threw up both hands. "Just laying out the facts…Captain."

His jaw clenched as he turned away from me.

"I didn't kill him," I said, but no one was listening.

e crew followed me from my quarters with mumbles and whispers, and my stomach churned. My crew'd gone from family to a maelstrom of accusations in less than forty-eight hours. A sweep of Jake's quarters turned up nothing more than the typical array of dirty laundry.

Lissa turned to Zac. "Where'd you get the idea to run salvage on this particular ship?" she asked.

His smile tightened at the edges. "We haven't had decent work in months. Not since…not since we took Seb on board. No one wants to deal with a vessel with an *Alphan*. Add in all that union crap—"

She waved her hand in the air. "Yes, yes, but how'd you find *this* job?"

"If we don't get more memory for the food replicators, we're gonna be eating like the junkies on Europa. When I saw this job come up on that board for folks looking for side-work, I figured it was a good fit. Ran it by Mark and off we went."

"Which board?" I asked.

I thought his lips would split, the painful way he over-grinned. "Side-Slide."

"Dammit, Zac.   at site's quasi-legal at best."

"Yeah, well, it ain't like you've never taken the odd job to keep *The Perffaith* running."

Lissa sighed. "Did you know the site is backed by Junto?"

"Yes."

e answer was too fast in coming, too confident. Lissa and Zac. Both with motive. Both my friends.

"You just happened upon a salvage job within hours of a fight?" asked Lissa.

"Well, yeah."

I stared at Zac. Every lie he told poked a hole in the façade of calm demeanor. I was drowning in lies.

"While we're speaking of weirdness," said Zac as the crew walked to his room. "Lissa, how'd the meeting go with Nick?"

e procession halted. "Ya knew our stiff?" asked Jake.

Lissa sighed. "Not really. I was investigating a murder—"

"So you've done this before then?" Zac smirked.

"Dammit, shut up and let me finish. I was investigating a mob hit and needed info from someone within the Family. *Zac*—" she stressed his name, "—gave me the email address for Mark's contact, a Nick Melorrey. I didn't know it was the same man, because I never met him in person. Never even had a video chat. Just emails."

"I'm sure that's all it was," said Zac.

When this was dealt with, I was gonna have a little chat with Zac. I didn't need more shit stirred on my ship.

Zac pressed his hand to his door's panel, and the lock released. "After you, Captain," he said.

Here was another room I'd visited many a time, though usually while piss-drunk. It was the only time he'd sucker me into playing a round of poker or jack.   e walls held holographic images of a dozen starships, each more decadent and expensive than *The Perffaith*. Like Petrie's room, his was neat leaning on not lived in.

I'd already skimmed each crew member's log, but I pulled up Zac's for another look while Lissa ri ed through the wall-drawers. Each log noted his entrance and exit from his room, none of which were particularly suspicious until the day of Nick's murder. At 08:00, he'd left his quarters for the morning. We'd all left the infirmary at 21:04, but the computer never logged Zac as returned to his room.

All of us were desperate for sleep, and knowing Zac, he'd have caught some zee-time when he could. I scrolled down and caught this morning's log. He'd left his room at 07:30.

Zac's shadow across the screen grew in size, and I closed the file. A few clicks later had me scanning his browsing history, emails, and calls.

"Feel free to enjoy my porn collection," he said and laughed. Gaps appeared in his history—moments where he'd logged into the system and done nothing. When I didn't laugh, his re ection on the screen frowned, and I forced a grin.

Something about the lack of computer data turned my stomach something fierce. In my study of the crew's logs, dozens of lines showed their movements and computer conversations in the past two days. Zac's were mostly the same except for the holes. "Zac, when did you come back to your room last night?" I asked.

"It must have been about 23:00 or so. Just after finishing my report. Actually, make that 23:15 since Lissa interviewed me toward the tail end of things."

He'd taken the bait. Now to drag the fish along until it stopped opping. "Something odd's going on with the computer. Between this and the scanners, I wonder "

Zac cocked his head. " ink we've been hacked or something?"

"Interesting choice of words coming from a former hacker," said Lissa. When I turned away from the computer, Lissa held Zac's scanner before her. Six heat sources read in his room. "I thought you said the scanner wasn't reading right," she said.

He shrugged. "It wasn't, but I replaced the memory this morning. Been reading just fine since then."

Lissa closed her mouth at my look. Last job we'd run had left our scanners blipping when they oughta have been blooping. Damned planetary moisture had done quite a number on their innards. I'd placed the order for new parts myself, only they hadn't arrived yet.

I didn't know why, but this was a bet I'd make sober. Zac was lying to me.

"Seb" by Raven Oak

CHAPTER ELEVEN

"Seems convenient," muttered Petrie from the doorway.

"What does?" Zac's voice was level, but he curled one hand into a half-fist.

"Your missing the heat source like that."

"Look, Petrie. I get that you're unusually gung-ho to find who killed Santa, especially if it takes the heat off of your girlfriend, but this don't mean shit. So I missed the heat source. With people blathering in their speakers at me, it's an easy mistake. Besides, Mark's dad died from CO poisoning. I still think he coulda jabbed himself with something when he felt himself go all woozy."

Seb brushed past Petrie. "Or maybe you are attempting to frame everyone for your own actions. You possess the needed knowledge to render the *Lucky Fish*'s computer silent."

"Maybe," said Zac, and he leaned nose-to-nose with Seb. "Or maybe you want it to sound that way. Since the murder, everyone's been hell-bent on accusing one another, but maybe it's just as I said. Here we are spinning our wheels over solving an accident when we could be selling our salvage. I don't know about you, Seb, but I'd like to eat something not replicated from old protein sometime this year."

Stress and lack of sleep had rendered them useless to me. I moved to step between the two, but Lissa beat me to it. "Enough," she shouted.

Before accusations started flying again, I said, "Everyone to their quarters. Let the skele-crew handle *The Perffaith*. And when I say your quarters, I mean your *own* quarters."

Petrie frowned but nodded.

"I've got to make sure the rest of the scanners are—"

I interrupted Zac with an upright hand. "I have a few leads to follow up before we finish grabbing salvage off the *Lucky Fish*. Stay in your room. Don't make me lock everyone inside."

My crew muttered as they spread out toward their quarters. Zac flopped into an empty chair, his fingers already running across the screen beside him.

"When this is all done, we're gonna have a talk, Zac."

"I'm sure," he muttered.

I followed Lissa outside and sighed when Zac's door shut behind me.

"You know something," she said.

"Possibly. Feel like helping?"

Lissa grinned and led the way to my quarters. Outside my door, she turned about-face. "I'm sorry. I should've told you about Melinda—"

"Don't," I said as I opened the door with a handprint. I locked the door behind us.

On the wall screen, I put in a call to Junto. Another hold as I waited for my message to reach the proper person, and Lissa fiddled with her sealed braid tips.

"Why are you calling him?" she whispered.

The screen twitched before Junto's mug popped up. "I thought I made it clear I don't owe you."

"You did, but I needed some information."

He furrowed his brows, then a slow smile spread across his face as he glanced over my shoulder at Lissa. "I see you two have worked things out."

I dismissed his attempts to push my buttons with a shrug. "Last time we had a chat, you said your boys were here to get the goods, yet they didn't. You and I both know you sent them to knock off Nick, but you had to ensure Nick was dead in the debris. Who'd you call on my ship to be sure?"

Junto's smile didn't falter as he wrested his attention from Lissa. "What makes ya think I did any such thing?"

"No games, Junto. If you had a mole in the Fam, you'd ush him out faster than I could toss the *Lucky Fish.* Allow me to do the same."

"What will you give me for such intel?"

It was my turn to smile. "I won't mention to the authorities where to find Melinda's killer."

"You won't, anyway. You got nothin'."

I pressed a button on my screen to forward a message his way. "In a few minutes, or maybe an hour with the way relays have been delayed, you'll get an email from Nick's email account—one where he makes very sure to state that he won't meet with Lissa here or tell her what happened to Melinda. I'm sure it could link Nick and you to her, which may open more doors than you want blown open at this point. Hell, they may find the clues in their own search of your computers there on Europa." I shrugged. "But hey, if you wanna take that risk, be my guest."

Junto's left eye twitched, but he gave the slightest nod. My account pinged. Guess he had faster mail relays than me. "Don't call again."

"I don't intend to."

 e screen darkened, and I pulled up the message he'd sent.   e decrypted file contained a series of video messages. Whoever our killer was had disconnected the video feed and fed the voice through the computer. A robotic voice read ff the details of the hit—where, when, who—not much else.

"Dammit," I muttered.

"Open another one."

Confirmation that Junto had told someone on board about the salvage and hired them to kill Nick *(if found)*, but nothing more. Another file, this one giving details of a meeting between Nick and Lissa. A meeting that never happened. At least according to her.

" at...that never happened. I didn't meet with him." She curled her fingers into fists. "You have to believe me."

"I can't."

"What are you going to do?"

"Find the proof I need. One way or another." My door slid open at my approach, and I gave her a brief nudge in its direction. "Look, just head back to your room. Stay put until I figure this out."

Lissa rested her hand against my chest—a moment's warmth in the situation's chill. "Mark—"

"Don't say it. We both know you wouldn't mean it in the morning."   e words were harsh, but I couldn't trust her. Not yet. I'd ask her forgiveness later, assuming I was alive to do it.

Assuming she wasn't the murderer.

My gut clenched as she left, and I pulled up the ship's map on the door panel. Heat sensors showed the two-member skeleton crew in place while the rest were in their rooms.

I sank into my cot and pressed the button to my right. A screen slid out, and I pulled up the logs from before.

e hole from last night was gone. Zac had altered his coming and goings again.   e question now was why. What was he hiding now? What had I missed? I pulled up the logs from the last twenty-four hours for Lissa's rooms, but they'd been cleared as well. He'd muddied the waters.

Maybe he was protecting Lissa. Maybe they were working together.

I scrolled away from the logs and into the command panel.   e computer's line to the derelict rang true enough, but the damaged ship wasn't singing back.   e *Lucky Fish* ignored my request to power up. Her computer was as lifeless as my father's corpse, which shouldn't have been the case. If nothing else, she could've piggybacked off our power.   e ship's black box was intact and should've been singing one last serenade.

Maybe if I brought the black box over to *The Perffaith*, I could get it talking. I grinned at my re ection in the screen.

But first, I needed to know if Lissa had met with my father.   e audio mentioned a meeting at a swank hotel in Garthus. Being all hoity-toity, maybe they'd have a record.

If I'd had to pinpoint the moment when the screen grew fuzzy, I wouldn't have been able. Only that as I stared at the small screen beside me, my vision rolled with my stomach. I blinked my way through the rocking long enough to pull up the article on carbon monoxide poisoning.

Damn.

So this was how it'd been done.

CHAPTER TWELVE

The room spun as I staggered to the door. The killer couldn't poison the entire ship without going down with us. If I could get to the hall— When I reached it, my door ignored my presence, and I pushed on the hand plate, which read:

LOCKED. OVERRIDE? Y/N

My finger slid across the Y, and the screen chirped a refusal. I tried to speak and couldn't. When birthdates and the names of family members didn't remove the lock, I blinked a few times while staring at the yellow glare. By the time I finished typing the L in Rachel, the world was a mix of gray haze and jagged edges.   e door slid open and fresh air smacked me in the face. As I fell to my knees in the hall, I made a mental note to send the ex-girlfriend a gift of some sort. Coughs ooded the hallway as crewmembers escaped their rooms.

Jake crawled his way over to me from his room across the hall. "Need to make…sure everyone…escaped."

I nodded, but my legs refused to lift me from the oor. Weak and quivering, I reached up and slapped my hand on a nearby panel. "Head count, please," I croaked.

Eight heat sources on board *The Perffaith*. "We're missing two."

Jake said, " e murderer. And his or her accomplice?"

"It appears to be the case." is time when I tried my legs, they held, though my stomach churned. "Check that everyone's okay. I need to get to the *Lucky Fish*."

Jake took the left corridor while I went right. Coughs covered what little could be said as I passed by my crew members. e stairwell's door shut behind me, and I took the stairs two at a time. Two ights down, salvage from the *Lucky Fish* lay scattered across the cargo bay. In the airlock chamber, two spacesuits were missing.

Dammit. e killer was going for the black box. e remaining evidence.

My legs quivered as I pushed one foot and then the other through the legs of a spacesuit, and my fingers trembled against the zipper pull. Part of me wished I had help—Lissa's help, to be honest—but for all I knew, she'd kill me rather than help me.

e zipper moved easier than I did. Fitting the helmet in place was a relief as cleaner oxygen swept through it, and I inhaled deeply a few times before sealing off the chamber for depressurization.

Two seconds into the derelict, goosebumps crept across my skin. Wasn't much reason for it—my lone light split across her darkness as expected—but a slim one foot of metal between me and the dark embrace of space set my wiggins-radar to off the charts, especially being alone with one, possibly two killers.

If the killer was smart, he—or *she*—would be hiding in a twist of metal wreckage. Maybe both of them were stupid, hiding out in the bridge. e idea made my steps slow as I shined my ashlight's beam into every shadow between me and the evidence I needed.

Dead ahead, the sliding doors to the bridge remained pried open from our previous excursion. e suit's emergency knife wobbled in my hand as I leaned my head around the doorway.

Nothing. e bridge was empty.

One oating lap around the bridge confirmed what my eyes told my brain. e main panel lay open, and I used the lip to pull myself beneath it. Its innards were an enigma to me, but I had a hunch the dead panel wasn't from damage. Not directly. I reached behind a mess of wires until I brushed up against the manual power switch. It was switched on.

Beside it lay the reset button. Once ipped, the black box's display lit up. Lights blinked and error codes scrolled across the three inch screen for a full minute before the command prompt blinked twice. Waiting.

I noted the killer's entrance by the pop of my speaker and gripped my knife. I couldn't ignore the cold sweat inside my suit.

Zac held one hand behind his back. A weapon of some kind? I used the panel for leverage as I faced him. "Was it you?"

He didn't answer—his eyes focused on the black box.

"Why?" I asked, and he pushed himself through the doorway and into the bridge.

Zac held an old-fashioned gun in his hand. "Money." He jerked the weapon to the right, and the speaker in my helmet crackled. "Get away from the box."

"Or what? You'll shoot me?" My breath came too fast. If he destroyed the black box, all evidence would die with me. "You're my best friend, Zac. I can't believe you'd kill me for money."

"Quit stalling. I saw you come alone. No one's coming to save you."

A bead of sweat crawled its way across my chin. Where was Lissa? Had she worked with him? Or had she been a hostage?

"How do you know that thing will even work?" I nodded at his gun. "No oxygen on the ship."

He rolled his eyes. "See? is is why. is!" e gun jumped with his gestures. "You don't have the brains to climb out of a paper bag, yet you're the mighty captain of his own ship. How many times have I pulled your ass from the proverbial fire?"

"More times than I can count. Which is why you've got me wondering what this is all about."

My helmet's speaker crackled again with his answer. "You. Here I've gone and done everything you've ever asked of me, saved your life any number of times, nursed your broken heart after that bitch dumped you, and how do you repay me? Hmmm? By making some bigoted *Alphan* your first officer!"

He wasn't working with Lissa? My breath caught in my throat. en where was she? I coughed in my helmet. Oh gods. Was she dead?

"Seb was an accident. I should've never accepted him from Junto."

Zac oated within a few feet of me. Spittle decorated the interior of his helmet, and his eyes were too large for sanity. "No shit. It should've been *me*!"

I held the knife uselessly at my side. "If you had a problem with me, why go after my father?"

Over his shoulder, a light ashed once in the corridor before fading. "I told you!" he shouted, and the gun jumped closer to my faceplate. " e money. Junto was willing to pay shiploads to make sure Nick was good and dead. You weren't going to miss him and with all that money, I'd be free of *The Perffaith*."

I tried to focus on his face rather than the new shadow in the hall, but the gun sent a new round of shakes through me. For whatever reason, Zac was convinced it would fire.

I held up my hands. "You were never a prisoner here, Zac. Take your money and go."

 e grin that split his thin lips was full of malice. "Can't. You know too much. How'd you figure out it was me, anyway?"

A booted foot stopped within the emergency doorway behind Zac.

 e silver strip across the helmet matched those across our feet. One of my crew was here. I sighed with relief, but Zac misread my reaction.

" at's it? is is all I get from the mighty captain of *The Perffaith*? So much for being perfect. What would your precious Gran think of you now?"

Anger ushed my face. Despite the lack of gravity, my arms and legs moved too fast through the dimly lit bridge. I reached for Zac as the pistol's muzzle ashed. Something hit me and pain erupted across my ribcage.

I ipped the latches of Zac's helmet, releasing the pressure seal. His mouth opened but whatever he said was lost with the lack of oxygen.

Lissa brushed past him. When she reached me, she slapped a glob of sealant across the hole in my suit. "Can you breathe? Did the bullet penetrate?"

My helmet occluded my view of my middle. "I don't think it

penetrated completely. Suit's too thick.   ough I think I bruised a rib or three."

As I spoke, she held up my arm to check gauges and sensor readings. "   e sealant should hold long enough to get you back on the ship, but we need to leave now."

"What about him?"

I didn't want to look at Zac. I stared at the   oor while my ribcage throbbed.

"Don't look," she whispered. "We need the black box."

Lissa tugged at my arm to get me moving. "Can you access it from *The Perffaith*?"

Zac's feet drifted past my view of the   oor. "Yes, now that its power is on."

We drifted through the *Lucky Fish*'s dark corridors in silence. My face grew warm as fog coated the interior of my helmet.   e airlock chamber stood ten feet at most, and my arm trembled as I pushed away from the wall.

"Liss…"

Her open mouth swam in the red tint of my vision, and I closed my eyes.

CHAPTER THIRTEEN

The overhead light doubled in brightness, and I winced. "Somebody do somethin' about that light," I said, or I tried to say, but the first few words were more a croak than actual speech.

"Sit tight, Captain. Sip this." Petrie placed a straw against my cracked lips.

e water burned going down, yet soothed the back of my throat.

is time when I opened my eyes, the light was less harsh, though my tear ducts worked overtime.

"What happened?" I asked. "Lissa—"

A hand squeezed mine, and when I turned my head, she sat beside me in the infirmary. Too many wrinkles lined her face. " e bullet didn't reach you, but it tore enough of a hole to cause problems."

"You patched it."

"Not enough.   ere was a pressure loss, enough that—" Her voice cracked, and she paused. "We almost lost you."

Several crew members waved at me from the view screen to my left. Petrie swiped them away and pulled up a list of numbers and diagrams. "Your blood was trying to boil its way out of your body," she said and injected something into my IV. "While the bullet didn't tear through the entire suit, you still bruised your ribs. You'll need to stay here overnight for observation. You're dehydrated and need the increased oxygen. "

"How long was I out?"

"A few hours. You came out of the hyperbaric tube half an hour ago."

Whatever she'd stuck in the line made the world prettier than I remembered, and I smiled at the fuzzy warmth.

" at's my Petrie-Dish." I tilted my head toward my security officer. "And my Lissa. Always looking out for me."

  e former smirked while the latter frowned.

I didn't care so long as they were both beside me.

CHAPTER FOURTEEN

"Careful now," Petrie said.

I waved her away. "Doc, I'm fine. All patched up. Walking and talking even." I allowed my legs to wobble, and many arms reached out to catch me.

When I laughed, Lissa lobbed a punch at my shoulder. "   at's not funny, Captain."

I chuckled harder as they escorted me to the common area. Everyone stopped outside the door, and Lissa waved her hand. "Captain's first."

   e door slid open, and when I stepped into the room, my eyes watered at the assault of lights. Greens and reds and whites twinkled, and a potted ivy sat in the corner. Someone, or perhaps several someones, had perched a   ameless candle in the pot. Some damned fool had painted the thing a merry set of red and green stripes.   e socks hanging across the wall were full of lumps and bumps, and a small box sat at the ivy's base.

"What's all this now?" I asked, and Seb grinned.

"Christmas!"

   ere was a hole in the wall where the shortest sock had been. Zac's. Lissa caught my frown and said, "We burned it, along with his body. While you were recovering, we blew up what remained of the *Lucky Fish.*"

My strength left me, and I stumbled. Jake shoved a chair under me, and I fell into it. "But—"

"Don't worry, we stripped her bare first. We got the black box data, too," she said and patted my arm. "It was a good haul all things considered. We should be able to get some fresh food at the next fueling station."

Seb picked up the small box and handed it to me. "Happy Christmas!"

Someone, probably Seb by the way he grinned, had bundled the box with a shirt and tied a silly knot at the top. My fingers fumbled with the thin rope until Lissa took pity on me and cut the fool thing.

"It is not fresh food, but perhaps you will find it equally enjoyable," said Seb.

Inside the box was the snow globe.

The twinkling lights overhead reflected off the flakes inside making them dance. I stared at it while my vision did a little dance of its own. "Damn dust on this ship. Time to cycle the air again," I said as I wiped my eyes with the back of my hand.

Lissa handed me a tissue. "We found it in…in Zac's quarters. We figured you'd want it, seeing how it was your father's."

"Thanks. What'd you find on the black box?"

The crew, who'd been digging through their "stockings" full of vitamin-candy, ceased moving at my question. Lissa took a deep breath and answered. "Junto admitted to paying Zac 500,000 credits to kill your father, though Junto wasn't the only one looking for him. He was wanted by the Family of Europa as well as crime syndicates in three other systems. Looks like this Santa thing was one of his covers. When Junto put out his request, Zac promised the Family he'd take care of him in exchange for the cash and a ship of his own."

"How'd you pull that info out of Junto?"

Lissa glanced at Petrie. "I made a deal."

I tried to stand and failed.

"I never said *I* wouldn't alert the authorities," she said and I laughed. "The black box contained brief notes from the captain of the

Lucky Fish. It seems he bought Nick's cover story and tried to protect him from Junto's boys. The captain hid him in that closet. Some protective shelter, I guess. It had its own oxygen system, which is how Nick survived post-battle. Gave him a shot of adrenaline to keep him going in the cold when the heat went out on the *Lucky Fish*. Junto's boys couldn't find him because their ship was too damaged in the fight."

I asked, "How'd Zac know about the request?"

"He's been on Junto's radar for a while. Managed to snake a long list of jobs out of Junto that were shunted our way so Zac could perform side-jobs for the Family. When we arrived at the *Lucky Fish*, he found a single life source on board. The one Junto said might be there. We had the new scanners, so we picked up what 'the boys' had not. Zac hacked the *Lucky Fish*'s computer and flooded the safe room with carbon monoxide."

Seb curled his hands into fists around his empty sock. "And while we were chasing salvage, he set the controller back to confuse the investigation. He may have succeeded had I not found the body."

"Junto knew we were in the sector, so it was the perfect opportunity to do what his boys had failed to do," said Lissa.

I swallowed the lump in my throat. "All this because he wanted to be First Officer. Felt like I'd slighted him."

"Is that what he told you?" Lissa asked.

I nodded.

"How did you deduce he was the murderer?" asked Seb.

"Little things weren't adding up. The scanner that suddenly didn't work when it did, the logs that were too perfect, the salvage job when we needed it most. The helmets crackling and such. We'd just replaced them— seemed weird to have them malfunctioning only when we needed to communicate most. I'm embarrassed to say this, but the black box of the *Lucky Fish* should have been a red flag. Even in a damaged ship, we should've been able to pull something from it, yet we got no response. Zac had cut all reserve power to it. I had to hit the manual reset button to restore it after reconnecting it. All the info from Junto helped point me in the right direction. Suppose I owe him for that."

I icked a peppermint across the table where it glanced off Petrie's arm. She stared at the cellophane wrapper a moment too long before she met my gaze. "He reproduced the methods and tried to kill us all in our rooms. Only two people on the ship could do that—the captain and—"

"—Someone able to hack the computer. Our killer," I said. Little piles of candy were strewn across the table, but we sat silently while the red and green lights made pretty patterns on the wall.

I stood up in a rush and clapped my hands together. "Look, Zac was bitter and angry about change. I don't know about you, but I can't spend my time looking over my shoulder for the what if 's and why's. No more jealousy and stalking people and the like. If you've gotta beef, say it. If you can't say it to me, say it to someone. We're supposed to be a family here."

My gaze crossed Seb's and he gave a brief nod of his head. He'd need watching still, especially if he was reporting back to Junto…

Jake grinned and held up a small ask. "I agree, Captain. I say we celebrate the holiday with a quart of my uncle's finest."

"Finest what?" Petrie asked as she sniffed the proffered container. "Is that intended to be drinkable?"

Jake set glasses on the table, and my medic poured a splash or two into each one.

"I propose a toast," said Seb, and he held up his glass. " at is what you do on Earth, is it not?"

 e crew laughed as five glasses glittered, though from the overhead lights or the uncle's alcohol, I couldn't say.

"A toast then," said Lissa. Several glasses clanked too early, and Jake held his side with one hand as he laughed. Desperation might have driven us to it, but under the programmed Christmas lights, we were alive and grateful. "To our captain, who brought us all together."

"And to Father Christmas!" Seb shouted.

"To Father Christmas," they echoed.

"Here's to you, Dad," I whispered.

 e booze burned like three suns going down, and Lissa hooted. "Happy Christmas indeed! You got any more of that stuff, Jake?"

"I do! My Christmas present to each of you, I guess."

"Did I ever tell you about how I met our great captain?" Lissa said.

I groaned.   ere wasn't enough hooch in the galaxy to keep my ears from burning through this story, but I grinned anyway and took another drink.

I was with the only family that mattered, and it was a happy Christmas indeed.

"Warp Speed" by Raven Oak

ABOUT OL' ST. NICK

Originally published in a holiday anthology entitled *Joy to the Worlds: Mysterious Speculative Fiction for the Holidays*, this story is one that I've always wanted to write. I have a thing for space-faring crews encountering old-world culture and tech.

I've always had a fascination with the absurd, which is probably why I enjoy British TV so much. When trying to think of a holiday story, I thought, what's more absurd than Santa being part of the Mob? Mob-Santa being murdered in space! Also, who hasn't had a holiday get-together with family that went horribly wrong?

I wrote this after reading *And Then There Were None* by Agatha Christie. I loved the idea of an enclosed space mystery, especially since they devolve into everyone pointing the finger at one another.

It's similar to "The Monsters are Due on Maple Street" by Rod Serling in that regard, which is another of my favorites.

What can I say? I've always enjoyed a good episode of *The Twilight Zone*.

"Ol' Nick" by Raven Oak

"Christmas in Space" by Raven Oak

PART IV

The Curse

"The Alley" by Raven Oak

CHAPTER ONE

"Yo, man, I told you the price was $75. What the hell is this shit?" I tossed the twenty onto the dirt at my feet. The punk didn't even have the gall to flinch, the little shit. "Get out of here with that garbage."

All five-foot-nothing, the kid puffed up his shoulders. "I can pay you back next week, man. Just hook me up, Simon. I'm beggin' you!"

I shook my head. "You know the rules. No cash, no product."

His shoes dragged across the dirty alleyway as he left, but my ears hardly registered the sound as a siren wailed nearby. I leaned against the brick wall as I sought the pistol at my waist.

Someone's steps running away, followed by others as the chase began. Little punk was gonna get busted. I moved further back into the shadows when something hard pressed against my back.

"Still dealing to kids I see."

The whisper was as hard as the gun, and I relaxed my shoulders. No need to fight yet.

"That punk ain't no child. I don't do that no more. But whatcha need? I can hook you--" Another shove with the gun, and I grunted. "Sure, my bad."

"You're bad all right. But tonight, it ends."

The shadow stepped sideways around me so I could see his face, and I froze. He was older, sure, but the eyes were the same. Sharp green and as cold as the night his kid had died. I put my hands up as he stared me down. "Look, I'm sorry 'bout what happened to your boy, but I ain't sold product to a kid since that night. I kept my promise. Things don't gotta go like this--"

"You thought I'd actually believe you? Your promises are as empty as my home these days. Now face the wall."

His badge clipped to his waistband flashed in the moonlight as he shoved me, and my face hit brick, leaving a trail of skin and blood behind. As I turned, a bright flash blinded me as his gun fired, then a sharp sting.

"Give my regards to my boy," the cop muttered, then silence.

I used to view time as the stretch between one fix and the next, a long string of highs and lows and too much and not enough money, but as I sat at my computer, time ticked by with a literal tick--a reminder that every second of every minute of every day was no longer my own.

It had been ten long years since my death, since I'd woken up in a cold room with nothing, not even my name.

They'd taken that from me first. Next they took every memory but the last. My death was something I dreamed about at night in the few hours' sleep I was allowed.

Was that really me? Had I been that callous and cold? Had I deserved to die? Those thoughts kept me awake more than the sounds from the workshop I slept above. My office resembled more closet and less office, but at least the room was heated by a corner fireplace, unlike the loft where I slept. The garish mash of faded reds and greens had stopped making my eyes water somewhere around the second year, and now they were little more than background noise, though the holly hanging in the corner still made me sneeze.

I returned to my computer where blueprints shuffled across the screen. New toy ideas for me to approve or deny before they were sent on to manufacturing. First a new soldier set followed by a poseable horse with real horse hair. The first I rejected--the world didn't need more soldiers--but the second sounded like something a kid would like...

"You rejected the Super-Soldier XP?"

Her voice cut through the workshop's chatter, and when her hand came to rest on my shoulder, I forced myself to relax rather than flinch.

"Too much violence out in the world to add to it," I said as I approved another toy.

"I agree, and I'm glad to hear you you've come around on this, Nicholas."

This time I did flinch. "I wish you wouldn't call me that. I had a name...before."

Well-manicured nails dug through my shirt to pierce my skin. "Before is of no importance to you, only the here and now. Focus on your work."

Her white hair touched my cheek as she leaned closer. A mix of cinnamon and vanilla tickled my nose as I fought back a sneeze.

"Now what do you say?" she asked.

"Thank you for your input, Mrs. Claus."

The door closed quietly behind her, and I shuddered.

When I wasn't approving and rejecting toys, my brain was kept busy with physical work. Mostly gluing together bits and pieces in order to create a toy some kid might like, assuming their parents didn't buy them some new downloadable doodad or another. Despite being busy, time crawled, but nothing like it did on *that* night--the one night a year I was permitted to leave. The one night I was forced to leave, if I'm being honest. The world out there held so little for a man with no name and no memories, though the world tried to give me both.

I might have been dead back then, but whatever magic she'd worked on me--the woman in the red cape--my body was alive now.

The first year I'd gone out, I found myself in a well-decorated bar. A child slept in one of the corner booths while her parents argued out back. It didn't matter what they were arguing about--I wasn't here for them--but she woke when a dish broke. Her eyes widened as she spotted me near the tiny tree, then her mouth opened as she saw the black bag I held.

"Are you him?" she whispered.

I'll be honest. Standing in a bar made me wish for a good drink and a pretty woman. As I said, my body was as alive as anyone else's. But here was this kid, asking me this question like I was some sort of god.

Something ethereal rested on my shoulder, and even though Mrs. Claus wasn't in the room, the squeeze was enough that I gasped for air like a fish out of water.

"Are you Santa Claus?" the child asked.

"I am."

Before she could ask anything else, another shout and broken glass rang out from the back room.

Don't get involved.

The number one rule of my job, and the second, don't get involved!

I stuck my hand inside the bag and pulled out a book. I never knew what would appear as the bag held a magic of its own, but when the child spotted the cover, her face lit up brighter than the neon closed sign flashing in the window. She took it from my outstretched hands like I handed her salvation, all interest in me lost.

In a blink, I was gone from the bar, my body traveling like lightning to the next location, which was a mystery as much as which gift went to which child. All those stories they tell you about being good or bad? It's all bullshit.

Honestly, most kids were innocent and good. Whatever I'd learned over the last decade, it was that the world made bad people. It didn't make bad kids. So on that one night a year, I went where I was told and handed out gifts like a good little Santa, all the while despising myself for turning away from the trauma and beauty of life.

It was early for me. It was all too easy to ignore the changing world outside the workshop when I only saw it once a year. When time stretched on infinitely, what did one night really mean?

I wasn't sure I cared to know.

"The Job" by Raven Oak

CHAPTER TWO

"What do you think of these?" Mrs. Claus held out a small pair of glasses. The frames weren't round like my own but resembled the shape of sunglasses as they wrapped around the face.

I held them before me and frowned. "Are sunglasses making a comeback?"

Her laughter reminded me of church bells, and I closed my eyes. When had I heard church bells? The memory slipped away as fast as it had arrived, and I ran a finger through my beard.

"They're not normal glasses, Nicholas. There's a company in the United States that's been trying, and failing I might add, to create these. Think of them as a combination of glasses, cellphone, and Internet combined."

"Remind me again, what does the Internet do? More of that downloadable stuff?"

She waved a hand at me. "Don't worry about that now. Just put them on."

When I set them on my face, the frames adjusted to better fit my large cheekbones. "They're comfortable, I'll give them that--" First they were normal lenses but a moment later, I was staring at my computer screen, toy designs and all. "Huh."

"Just tell it what you want it to do."

"Um, glasses, hello. Approve toy." The design in front of me slid aside and another toy took its place. "So, it's like a computer?" I asked.

"And more. You can make phone calls on it, play games in 3D, do research, and read books. Basically anything you can think of."

I removed the glasses and handed them back. "I think those will be a big hit with the boys. Both hands free and all."

Her otherwise cheery face was marred by a scowl. "Really? That's the first thing that comes to mind?"

At least this time she didn't grip my shoulder. Some days it almost felt like we'd known each other an eternity as partners rather than employer and employee, forced though that role might be. Instead, she continued to scowl as she broke the glasses in half.

"Rejected," she muttered as she left my office.

I couldn't help but grin.

Years passed into decades of servitude, and the reminders of my curse became fewer and far between as I grew to accept my role in this new world. The toys changed, as did the children, but the world remained the same. People killing others, greed controlling...well, everything, and climate change making my one night a year a chaotic ride.

Sometimes it was too hot for the red suit custom built for my large frame, but I wore it all the same. Christmas wouldn't be Christmas without it. I followed the rules and did what I was told, but sometimes, I allowed myself a moment or two to take a long look at the world around me.

Gone were the small screen televisions of my youth, the clunky phones with cords that wrapped around your feet as you talked, and the radios as big as my head. I couldn't figure out how I remembered those objects any more than I recalled the bits and pieces of memories that leaked out in my dreams--images of drug deals gone bad, of people I'd hurt. People probably long dead as time lost all meaning.

Everything was smaller. Faster. Brighter.

If I watched the world for too long, I got lost as my body fell through the seconds like sand in an hourglass.

But I tried. Oh, I tried.

Something inside of me demanded it, so every year, I picked one child to focus on. That delivery became special as I asked my questions and gleaned what intel I could from the world, information otherwise forbidden to me as I pushed aside the number one rule.

That year, whatever year it was, I found myself in a cornerstone home in New York City. The fireplace's embers cast an eerie glow in the living room, and while the furnishings shouted poverty, the tree in the corner glowed with a brightness that lit the room with love. Surely there were children here or else the magic that drove my sentence wouldn't have brought me to this home, so I tucked my hand inside my bag and found two gifts to tuck under the tree.

The pull of magic was strong and tried to tug me from the home, but I ground my teeth. Something eerily familiar pulled me in the other direction, and I set off down the hall to explore the home further. Just past a tiny kitchen and dining room lay a bathroom and an empty bedroom. The next room held a sleeping child who didn't even twitch when I opened the door. The final bedroom lay before me and my stomach lurched.

Why was I nervous?

When I opened the door, a king sized bed stood across the room from me and in it, an old man slept. His gray beard covered most of his face, and when I stepped forward, his eyelids snapped open.

Green eyes. No matter how many wrinkles surrounded them, I would have recognized them in any light.

The coldness in them remained as he stared at me.

"You know who I am?" I asked.

He sat up, arms shaking with great effort, and he beckoned me forward.

"No," I whispered. *Don't get involved.* It didn't matter what I wanted, something urged me forward and my feet only stopped once I stood before the bed, my knees knocking against the bedframe.

"I know you, Nicholas, and you are no saint."

The voice crackled like the room's fireplace, and I flinched. "That's not my name."

"It is now. How do you like your servitude thus far?"

It made no sense. How could he know? I glanced at him and for a moment, the old man vanished, leaving behind the young cop who'd shot me. "How--?"

The young father shifted back to the old man, who tugged his blankets closer to his shoulders as if to protect himself from a cold that didn't chill the room. He opened the palm of his hand and in it lay a silver button, old but polished like new. "It is the curse of this button. I wasn't even sure it would work, but the woman promised it would."

"What woman?"

"She was older, white hair, and a laugh like chiming bells."

He continued to describe her but all sound had dropped away as I stared at him. Mrs. Claus. She was behind the curse.

The cop grabbed my gloved hand. "I've had a long time to think on what I did. Even longer to think of my son and what he would've wanted, and I know it wasn't this. It's my time, but I'd not have my grandson suffer. Would you stay with him, at least until his mother arrives?"

"You have a grandson?"

He nodded. "I didn't know until after I'd... Anyway, I'd rather he not be alone when he wakes as I won't be here."

"What do you mean?"

"The woman who gave this to me, she promised I'd only see you again on my death bed and so it must be. My time. Promise me he won't be alone."

"I-I promise." When I uttered the words, something inside me snapped. No matter how much I wished to flee the room, I wouldn't be leaving until I kept my word.

His eyes softened for a moment as he lay back further into his pillow. "I'm sorry for what I did, kid. No matter what you did, no one deserves death. It wasn't my job to play judge, jury, and executioner. She said the curse was permanent, but maybe this will have some meaning."

He pressed the button into the palm of my hand and took a slow, dragged breath. "I forgive you."

As his chest rose and fell once more, I clutched the button in my hands. I was a bad man. A horrible man. Memories came rushing back as if they'd never been gone. His son, the drugs I'd sold him, his overdose, and how I'd gone right on dealing as if the kid's death was nothing more than an afterthought.

I glanced up and the cop was no more, his chest still in the night.

"Grandpa?"

The voice from the doorway was young, and when I turned around, he grinned.

"Santa!"

The little boy made to rush forward and I met him halfway, catching him in my arms before he could spot his dead grandfather. Bad enough this holiday would be forever marred by loss, but he didn't need the gruesome picture.

"Let's go see what's under the tree, shall we?" I asked.

"But what about grandpa?"

"He'll join us in a little bit. Allow him to rest for a while longer."

I carried the boy into the living room and set him in front of the tree. As he grinned over his presents, a key turned in the lock and a short, fair-haired woman entered. The lines around her eyes and mouth tugged at her good looks, and she gasped when she spotted me.

"What are you doing here? Who are you?"

I stepped into the light where she could better see the outÿt I wore, but her eyes remained wary. "I am Nicholas. I...I came to see your father-in-law. He asked me to keep an eye on your son until you arrived."

"No. I know who you are...Simon."

Had that been my name? Of all the memories that returned, my name had remained unspoken until now. Something about her tone's sharpness drew the boy to his mother, where she placed a hand on his shoulder. He squirmed beneath her tight grip.

"Mama, you're hurting me!"

She pushed him toward the hallway as she rooted around in her purse for something. "Go to your room."

Her eyes never left mine as the living room shifted, the magic pulling me away before she found what she was looking for.

Another living room greeted me, and I made myself useful laying presents beneath a tree without looking. I moved on autopilot as my brain spun in circles. My name is Simon.

Or was it? I certainly wasn't the same man from that alleyway, but who was I? Nicholas had been thrust upon me by a curse. It wasn't a name or a role of my choosing.

The rest of the evening was a blur, and it wasn't until I stood in the workshop's loft that my mind stood still long enough to realize the cop might have forgiven me, but the woman hadn't.

I would have to do something about that. After all, I had an eternity to do so.

"Waiting for Santa" by Raven Oak

CHAPTER THREE

I was back to my job of approving toys when Mrs. Claus walked in, a certain twinkle in her eyes that meant she was either in a good mood or I was in trouble. I leaned back in my chair and felt the warmth rise to my cheeks. The way the red of her dress fit her shape made me smile in a way I hadn't before.

Over the years, I'd grown used to her ways, not to mention the job. It wasn't so bad what I did. If it could bring joy to millions of children all over the world, what better job could there be? Certainly better than slinging drugs on the street corner, that was for sure.

When she rested her hand on my shoulder, I leaned into it. "What can I do for you, Mrs. Claus?"

"It's almost that time again."

Something about the way she said it, the way her words staggered across her tongue, made my heart seize up. "You seem sad about it. Come on, it's almost Christmas," I said with a laugh.

While she smiled in response, the joy didn't reach her eyes. "Well, yes, I suppose I am a bit sad. Sometimes the season hits me differently." Her hands were cold when they stroked my bearded chin. "I remember when you first arrived here. You found my touch fearful."

"I still do!" I said as I caught her hand before she could pull it away. "Any witch who puts such a curse on a man is someone to be fearful of, don't you think?"

"Indeed! Still, there's so much to do. Are you ready for next week? I think this might be our best season yet."

I wrapped my arms around her waist. "I agree, but until then, I think I have time for a little mischief. How about you?"

There was that sadness again in her smile. She nodded, her throat convulsing as if she couldn't speak. Whatever it was that drove her melancholy was pushed aside as she kissed me.

I'd ask her about it later, if we had the time. Perhaps after the holiday rush...

One more present under one more tree.

I turned to leave when something tugged me toward the home's window. Below, snow cast shadows across the city, but one shadow in particular lay darker and deeper than the rest. Rather than allow the magic to pull me away, I left the home through the front door and made my way towards the alleyway ahead.

Two men stood close together, one whispering frantically in the other's ear. The way the younger shouldered the other, my gut told me something was about to go sideways, and I stepped into the darkened alley.

"Please, I'm begging you! Just a bit, to take the edge off man!"

The elder of the two tilted his head and ran his fingers through his slicked back hair. "You know the rules. No cash, no product."

The hair on my arms stood up beneath my red suit as my mind assaulted me with memories, but I pushed them aside. The past couldn't help me now. I cleared my throat, and the elder jerked his head in my direction.

"Yo, get lost *Sant-ey* Claus. This is a private meetin'."

When I touched the young man's shoulder, he jumped. "I don't think you need this in your life. It's Christmas. Perhaps you should go home?"

Magic stirred in the air, swirling around the kid's head before it landed on him like a gentle breeze. He gave a twitch when it touched him, then turned around and fled.

"Man, you just cost me a client! Whatcha gonna do to make it up to me?"

I reached out toward him but stopped when I spotted the gun. He pointed it at me with trembling hands.

"How old are you, kid? Nineteen?"

He glared at me, his chin raised in defiance.

"Nineteen it is then. Look, is this how you want to spend the rest of your life? Looking over your shoulder for the cops and trading one fix for the next?"

"Don't think I won't shoot you!" he yelled.

I'd managed to get within five feet of him when he cocked the revolver. Having been shot to death, it wasn't an experience I wished to repeat, but maybe the magic would protect me. Funny how I'd never thought to ask the missus about that...

I stuck my hand in my fur lined pocket and removed the button I'd placed there too many years ago.

The kid's eyes narrowed when he saw it. "My grandpa had a button like that. Said it brought him good luck."

Wait, was this... "He gave it to me that night, you know. The night he forgave me."

"Wait, you knew my gramps?" His eyes narrowed. "I-I remember you. My ma called you Simon. Said you killed my dad."

"Drugs killed your dad, kid, but yeah, I helped him to it. Same as you're helping others to it now."

"You here to talk me into cleanin' up my life?"

I held the button out to him and when he touched it, pain ripped through me like I hadn't felt since that night. My bullet ripped through chest all over again, and I hovered above my body for a moment as my clothes dissolved. Beside me, the kid screamed in pain or frustration, maybe both as the Santa suit enveloped him.

In his hand, the button pulsed in rhythm to his heartbeat for a few seconds before he disappeared, the magic taking him elsewhere.

All the magic that had carried me dissipated, leaving behind the shell of an old ghost.

As I floated beside my corpse, the air hummed and Mrs. Claus appeared. She walked up to my body and touched a hand to its cheek. When she looked up, rather than seeing through me, she met my gaze. "Simon, it's time for you to rest."

She hadn't called me Nicholas.

I opened my mouth to speak but no sound came out, and she nodded confirmation. My sentence was served, and now someone else would take up the mantle of Santa Claus. I could swear tears welled up in my eyes, but when I touched them, my skin was dry.

I made to reach for her, this woman I'd grown to love, but she stepped back with the shake of her head.

"Go. Rest now, my love. Let someone else carry this weight."

Something else tugged at me, something I couldn't resist even if I'd tried. Her figure grew smaller as I was pulled further away.

As I closed my eyes, the world around me disappeared one last time.

"Help Me" by Raven Oak

ABOUT THE CURSE

Anytime I think about people who serve others, be they wait-staff, chauffeurs, or volunteers, I've always wondered how much they enjoy what they do. If given the option (and finances weren't a consideration), would anyone willingly choose to serve others for a living? Especially considering how many people treat those who serve?

We always hear about Santa Claus being a benevolent creature who loves children and loves creating toys for them, but after thousands of years at this, surely even Santa Claus needs time away. As much as I love writing, if I had to spend eternity creating stories, I'd grow to hate it. I think it would become a chore and more of a curse rather than the joy that it is now.

From this came the idea of Santa's identity itself being an actual curse. What if it was a punishment for doing something wrong, and rather than Mrs. Claus being his jovial wife and partner, if she were the one meting out his eternal-long punishment? From there, the story told itself in my head. I only had to type it up.

"The Bar" by Raven Oak

"'Til Death Do Us Part" by Raven Oak

ACKNOWLEDGMENTS

I would like to thank the many people whose hands touched these stories in some way, including my editor and the many alpha and beta readers who gave great feedback. Also, my partner, who is by far the best early draft editor a writer can have.

I would also like to thank Mr. MacKenzie, my art teacher from middle school, who told me I had a talent in my hands. He encouraged me to draw and create, even when I didn't think it mattered. It took a long time for me to realize he was right. R.I.P., Mr. Mac.

Many thanks go to my good friend, Elise, who always encourages me in my endeavors; my best friend, Mary, who is both inspiring and a great ear when I need to vent about home improvement or medical hell; my good friend, Jennifer, who kicks my butt when I don't write enough; and again, my partner in all things, Erik.

Without my posse, I'm not sure I would've survived these last three crazy years. Thank you. <3

ABOUT THE AUTHOR

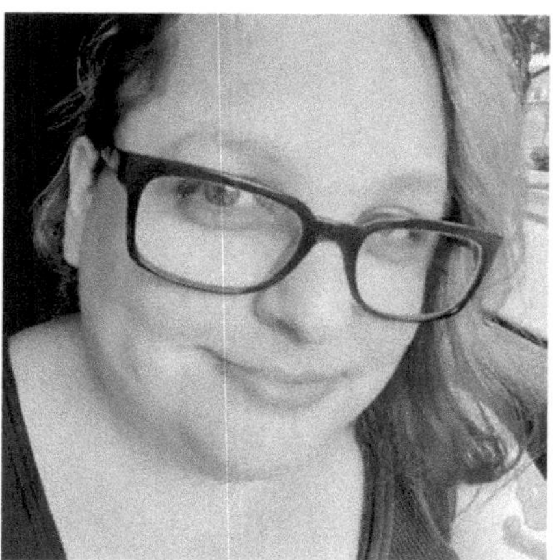

Photo by St. Photography Studios

Multi-international award-winning speculative fiction author Raven Oak is best known for ***Amaskan's Blood*** (2016 Ozma Fantasy Award Winner, Epic Awards Finalist, & Reader's Choice Award Winner), ***Amaskan's War*** (2018 UK Wishing Award YA Finalist), and ***Class-M Exile***. She also has many published over a dozen short stories in anthologies and magazines. She's even published on the moon! (No, really!) Raven spent most of her K-12 education doodling stories and 500 page monstrosities that are forever locked away in a filing cabinet.

Besides being a writer and artist, she's a geeky, disabled ENBY who enjoys getting her game on with tabletop games, indulging in cartography and art, or staring at the ocean. She lives in the Seattle area with her partner, and their three kitties who enjoy lounging across the keyboard when writing deadlines approach. Her hair color changes as often as her bio does, and you can find her at **www.ravenoak.net**.

You can *Join the Conspiracy*, her official mailing list to gain information and freebies at http://www.ravenoak.net/for-readers/mailing-list/ Besides her website, Raven Oak can be found online at the following:

Facebook: facebook.com/authorroak
Facebook Reader Group: https://www.facebook.com/groups/ravenconspiracy/
Twitter: twitter.com/raven_oak
Instagram: instagram.com/author_raven_oak
Goodreads: goodreads.com/raven_oak
YouTube: youtube.com/user/kaonevar
LinkedIn: https://www.linkedin.com/in/ravenoak1
BookBub: bookbub.com/authors/raven-oak
Amazon Author Page: https://www.amazon.com/Raven-Oak/e/B00P5PT4AM

ALSO BY RAVEN OAK

<u>The Boahim Universe</u>

Amaskan's Blood

Amaskan's War

*Amaskan's Honor**

*Ear to Ear**

<u>The Xersian Struggle Universe</u>

*The Eldest Silence**

Class-M Exile

<u>Stand-Alone Works</u>

Dragon Springs & Other Things

Space Ships & Other Trips

Ol' St. Nick

The Ringers

From the Worlds of Raven Oak: A Coloring Book

Hungry

The Loss of Luna

Peace Be With You Friend

* Forthcoming

LIKE WHAT YOU'VE READ?

Word of mouth is the number one **best** way to ensure that your favorite authors have continued success—better than any paid advertisement.

If you enjoyed this book, please consider leaving a **review** or starred ranking on Goodreads, bookstore websites, and other retail or reviewer sites.

Your review is greatly appreciated.

www.ingramcontent.com/pod-product-compliance
Lightning Source LLC
Chambersburg PA
CBHW052014190726
48295CB00012BA/638